CW00433108

SILVER MOON

GREAT NOVELS
OF
EROTIC DOMINATION
AND SUBMISSION

NEW TITLES EVERY MONTH

www.smbooks.co.uk

WRITE TO;
SILVER MOON READER SERVICES;
Suite 7,
Mayden House,
Long Bennington Business Park,
Newark NG23 5DJ

YOU WILL RECEIVE A FREE MAGAZINE OF EXTRACTS
FROM OUR EXTENSIVE RANGE OF EROTIC FICTION
ABSOLUTELY FREE. YOU WILL ALSO HAVE THE CHANCE
TO PURCHASE BOOKS WHICH ARE EXCLUSIVE TO OUR
READERS' CLUB
***
NEW AUTHORS ARE WELCOME
Please send submissions to;
The Editor; Silver Moon books
Suite 7, Long Bennington Business Park
Newark NG23 5DJ

Tel: 01400 283 488

Copyright 2009
This edition published 2011

The right of Sean O'Kane to be identified as the author of this book has been asserted in accordance
with Section 77 and 78 of the Copyright and Patents Act 1988. All rights reserved.

ISBN 978-1-907475-35-1

All characters and events depicted are entirely fictitious; any resemblance to anyone living or dead is entirely coincidental

THIS IS FICTION. IN REAL LIFE ALWAYS PRACTISE SAFE SEX

GIRL SQUAD

by

Sean O'Kane

CHAPTER 1

"Number One and keep the skirt up."

Amelia read the text message and smiled happily. The incoming message alert had sounded, muffled through the fine kid leather of her handbag, just as she was leaving work early and now she stowed the phone again, closed her office door and walked along the plushly carpeted corridor of TPI Fund Management Ltd. and went into the Ladies' toilet.

Once safely in a cubicle she set her bag on the lid of the toilet and hoisted her short tweed skirt up to her hips and with her thumbs pushed her black lace thong down her thighs and then bent, pushed them right down to her ankles and shook free of her feet, then she picked them up and put them beside the bag. She had been pretty certain that morning that her master would text her at about this time and so she had not worn the thick tights she would normally have on a cold autumn day and instead had come to work bare legged. It had been a chilly and bracing start to the day but now at least she didn't have to struggle with the wretched things to obey her order.

With her skirt rucked up out of the way she spread her legs and began to perform Number One.

This involved using her right hand to gently ease its way between the delicate fronds of her inner lips and to begin to rub at the prominent nub of her clitoris itself until it erected. Then she would slide her hand further under her and, still rubbing with the palm of her hand insert two and then three of her fingers into her vagina. The receipt of the text message coupled with the fact that she was on her way to see her master had done the initial groundwork for her and her clitoris was already throbbing and hard whilst her vagina was hot and moist as soon as her fingers entered it. She shivered as the first spears of pleasure pricked through her. But biting her lip to concentrate, she began the second part of the order.

"Every part of my body belongs to my Master. Even my thoughts are his. I may have no secrets from him, just as no part of my body is hidden from him," she recited to herself. She was required to do this ten times for a Number One. Her master knew she had a long way to drive and so hadn't ordered a Three, or worse in terms of carrying on normal life, a Four which required the recitation to be made forty times. She always found it hard to concentrate and get the right number of recitations with her hand rubbing her clit – the fingers inside her were purely because her master liked to know she had put them there – the real damage was done by the fact that she couldn't be gentle with her clitoris even if she wanted to be; not while she was under his orders.

Dimly she heard the next cubicle being used and tried to stifle her breathing which was becoming ever more ragged as she ground herself mercilessly. She was pretty certain she was on her fifth recitation now.

".....just as no part of my body is hidden from him."

Yes, it was definitely the fifth and she went on to complete the sixth. The cubicle next door emptied and she breathed a sigh of relief and rubbed even more fiercely.

She closed her eyes and leaned against the wall as she started the seventh, her mind beginning to whirl away on visions of his face, his hands on her breasts, his whip stinging her back, his hand working her tight sheath amid all her outpourings as she waited to be possessed and used for his pleasure.

She bit her lip hard and started on her eighth, trying desperately to concentrate on each word as she felt her legs weaken. The door of the cubicle behind her closed as someone entered it and saved her by dragging her up from drowning in sensations and memories – and expectations of the next week to be spent with her master. She finished her ninth and started the final recitation with a soft growl of determination to really punish her clitoris as she ground out the words in her head.

Once she finished she had a moment's struggle against her own inclination to continue for just a few seconds and see if she couldn't bring herself off but the thought of the drive ahead finally forced her hand away from the hot and wet confines of her groin and she sagged against the wall, thanking her master for being cruel enough to always remind her of her subservience to him without making her normal life completely impossible, which he could so easily. After all, he knew she would obey any command he gave her.

After a few moments she stood up properly, wiped herself clean, straightened her skirt, picked her thong off the cistern and popped it into her bag – a Number One meant going knickerless from then on – and hoping she didn't look too flustered, she flushed the toilet and went out to repair her look in the mirror that ran the whole length of the wall above the sinks.

After brushing her hair, applying blusher and just a tad more lipstick, Amelia Johnson appraised herself before setting off to see her master for a whole glorious week. She was in her late twenties with thick, dark hair that fell to her shoulders, her eyes were wide-set and large; dark brown and lustrous. Her face was often described as elfin, narrowing from its wide brow to an almost sharp chin below a wide and generous mouth with shapely and full lips. Her torso was slender but supported breasts that were quite adequate if not exactly big, but they sported nipples that were definitely big and charmingly tip-tilted as well.

Where she was going she knew that there were plenty of men, apart from her master, who knew how to enjoy themselves with nipples like that. The thought reignited the warmth between her naked thighs and she quickly distracted herself by collecting her things together and beginning the brisk walk from the office to the tube and the journey to the over ground station where she had left her car. She just made it before the Friday rush hour kicked in in earnest and so she didn't have the torment of being pressed against other bodies while being acutely aware of her state of undress. At least she could get a seat and sit with her legs demurely pressed together until it was time to change to an over ground train for two stops and then retrieve her BMW for the drive down to Berkshire. She had to wait until the interior light in the car faded before she could start off because her master had decreed one last humiliation and once she was in darkness, with a practised lift of her bottom and a quick heave on her skirt, she complied with the final part of her order – to keep her skirt raised. The cream leather of the upholstery was quite chilly for a while but from past experience, Amelia knew that as she neared her destination, she would be extremely hot and wet and would certainly leave an embarrassing mark on the pale leather. Her master knew that as well.

She joined the flow of the traffic on the M4 heading west out of London, streams of tail lights in the twilight making a river of jewels that swept her towards her destination.

By the time she turned off the motorway it was fully dark and the last few miles along country roads had been slow going. But at last she was able to swing the car off the road, swipe her card through the recognition system that now governed the great wrought iron gates and, once they had swung ponderously open, drive through them onto the long avenue that led to The Lodge; the most prestigious and secretive SM club in the land. However for the last three years of its existence it had not only offered the most beautiful and submissive Housegirls for its members' use, it also hosted in its extensive parklands the CSL stable where some of the finest female gladiators to grace the modern arenas were trained.

Amelia's master was assistant trainer there and she herself acted as a groom when she visited him. Now, as the car's headlights picked out the trunks of the great lime trees on either side of the drive, her naked vagina began to lubricate and she was uncomfortably aware it was drizzling its juice onto the leather seat, but the prospect of returning to The Lodge and CSL, with all that that entailed, was one she was helpless to resist.

She slid her car into a space in the car park that stretched out in front of the great house itself and got out, noting with chagrin that indeed she had left a damp patch on the driver's seat and that the wind was now blowing coldly up her skirt and rapidly cooling her ardour. She shivered and scuttled round to the boot to retrieve her case and then hurried across to the sweeping stone staircase that led up to the front doors, she ran up and pushed one of them open. Within was a tall lobby with fishing waders, golf bags and umbrellas tossed carelessly on either side. Testimony to the fact that the members enjoyed pursuits other than just SM during their stays. Amelia walked towards the etched glass doors at the far end, enjoying the feel of the maleness the room exuded before stepping through into the warmth and light of The Lodge proper.

In the great hall the chandeliers cast a brilliant light on the rich carpeting and the ornate staircases, and on the portraits and landscapes that adorned the walls. The girl on reception looked up with a beaming smile as the door closed behind Amelia, shutting out the weather, the dark and the outside world. She took a moment to just stand and breathe in the atmosphere of wealth – expensive cigars and wax polish - delicious cruelty and mind-blowing sex that pervaded the air of the house. A group of men in dinner jackets wandered across, heading for one of the lounges for a drink before dinner. One of them spotted her and came across, smiling broadly.

"Miss Johnson! What a lovely surprise! If Brian and Carlo can spare you, I'd love to spend a couple of hours in a dungeon with you, I don't mind which one," he said and then took her hand to kiss it with grave courtesy.

"Thank you Mr Gresham. If you mention it to them I'm sure they'll make the necessary arrangements," she replied bobbing a Housegirl curtsy.

The man laughed. "I'm sure they will!" he said and strolled back to rejoin his colleagues. Amelia went up to the reception desk and signed herself in, the girl behind the desk was one she vaguely remembered from her last visit, like all the Housegirls she was dressed in a satin evening gown that was cut very low – almost to the point of displaying the areolas of her breasts – and Amelia knew that the full, pleated skirt of the dress was slit at the back so that the wearer could be groped perfectly easily by any of the members. This particular girl was black haired and her make up carefully complemented the red gown she wore.

She greeted Amelia in English which was grammatically perfect but spoken with a pronounced accent and Amelia recognised that she was an owned Housegirl, a girl who had been bought at auction by the club. Some of the girls were owned by members and leased to the club either while the master stayed or while he was absent – maybe out of the country – pursuing business or different pleasures, but the majority were bought and owned directly by the club.

Amelia picked up her case and made for the small door that led off the back of the hall and into the world of 'below stairs'.

The kitchens were their usual mad maelstrom of steaming pots, hissing and flaming pans and frantic, shouting chefs creating culinary masterpieces for the discerning palates of the members who regularly dined at the finest restaurants in the world and expected near-perfection in everything about them. Housegirls assigned to domestic duty for the evening meal rushed in and out as they laid tables in the dining room and prepared to begin serving. Some of them flashed quick, bright smiles of recognition at her as she hurried through, anxious not to be in the way. She stepped out from a side door into the old stableyard. This was where the pony girls were kept for as long as a member wanted them stabled. Amelia had known some girls dumped by their masters as ponies for as much as a month, while they were off somewhere else. Mostly though, it was just for a week or a few days at a time and the grooms were Housegirls themselves and could easily find themselves harnessed and stabled at a member's whim.

Tonight there was a pleasantly busy atmosphere from the stable block opposite. Light flooded out from the door to the main stables and threw a wide beam across the cobbles. Buckets clanked as stalls were washed out and floors were mopped, a Housegirl hurried across with a big urn that had had the ponies' supper in it before it had been emptied into the troughs, and as Amelia turned left and walked towards the arch that led out into the park, she could hear the grooms laughing and joking amongst themselves. Madame Stalevsky, the formidable ex-ballerina who trained and oversaw all the girls would be along shortly to inspect the stalls before lights out and that would settle them all down until the inevitable creeping between beds began. The threat of a beating if they were discovered only made the furtive explorations and orgasms all the more appealing.

Beyond the arch Amelia hurried along as the chill bit at her again and took a path on the right, illuminated by lamps standing in the shrubbery. Up ahead a large, unlit structure blocked out the stars.

When she reached it she groped for the door handle and lifted the heavy latch using both hands, then she let herself in, retrieved her case and closed the twelve foot high door before looking around her. The light was harshly neon and ahead of her she could hear men's voices and among them was her master's. The steel structure amplified and distorted the voices but she would know him anywhere. There was the occasional smack of a whip and the sound of feet shuffling on sand or sawdust. This was where she really belonged, she thought, walking forward eagerly, past the dark green painted, luxurious horsebox with the letters CSL in gold italics on its side. On either side of her, banks of seats sloped steeply down to what the building's designers had intended to be an equestrian arena. The seats were empty now, as those Lodge members who had been watching had gone to change for dinner and the arena slaves were finishing their day's training. Amelia pushed open the low door in the boarding that surrounded the arena and walked in.

Her master was just a few feet away on her left and standing behind an imposingly built, naked, black girl who was bent forwards, her upper chest resting on the top of the boards, her legs straight and spread, her hands clipped together at her back. She was running with sweat despite the cold evening, and even her dark skin could not entirely disguise the network of fine welts that laced her back, ribs, buttocks and thighs.

Brian, her own master, had a clipboard laid on the slave's back and was conferring with a younger man – the new assistant trainer, Tony, who was holding a long driving whip consisting of a thin, flexible pole with a length of stiff whipcord depending from its end. Amelia knew exactly what she was witnessing. The two men were deep in conversation about the figures on the clipboard, which would be times for how fast the slave had pulled a single seat trap over measured distances.

As the slave in question was Fiji – a Polynesian girl bought at auction a few months previously – Amelia knew Tony would have been running her over quarter and half mile tracks. She was built for endurance rather than sprint speed and when she wasn't racing, she formed part of CSL's formidable whip melee team with two other slaves; Ox and Trouble.

As she watched, Brian smacked the slave on her haunch as one might pat a horse after a good gallop, Tony took the clipboard and went back into the arena, Brian meanwhile unzipped his flies and tugged his rampantly erect cock out. It had been some weeks since they had last been together and Amelia's throat went dry at the sight of the magnificent purple dome that she sometimes still struggled to contain in her mouth.

He used one hand to bend the shaft slightly downwards and then slipped it between the dark-skinned slave's thighs and moved forwards until his pelvis rested against her buttocks. Amelia watched fondly as the slave's body adjusted to the penetration and she began a spectacular gyration of her hips to enjoy her trainer's cock within her, she swallowed and her thick tongue ring rattled against her teeth.

Amelia adored the ease with which her master took his pleasure with any slave that took his fancy, or which needed a reward. And increasingly she envied the slaves their constant availability.

She put her case down and went to join her master.

Brian looked over and smiled at her as she approached.

"Hi. Good journey?" he said, perfectly unabashed at being up to the hilt in a squirming and humping slave in front of her. As was perfectly right and proper in Amelia's eyes.

"Not bad thanks," she replied, leaning on the slave's back and giving her master a kiss. "She still a good fuck?"

"Yep. One of the best!"

They both took a moment to admire the athletic way in which Fiji was bending her spine back and forth and rolling her fabulous buttocks against Brian's pelvis. Amelia folded her arms and leaned fully on the slave's back, craning her head towards her master's crotch as she lowered herself and watching eagerly as an inch or so of his shaft was revealed when Fiji alternated her swivels with humps and hollows of her back, something she continued to do in spite of Amelia's weight. Gentle groans of pleasure and more teeth-on-tongue-ring rattles came from her head as Amelia unfolded one arm, reached underneath the slave and began to knead a heavy, warm handful of breast.

Brian held himself quite still and let the slave do the work, his hands just keeping a steadying grip on her haunches.

"Got a hell of a grip on her!" he said. "Some of the members reckon she's better than Blondie or Ayesha in that department."

He leaned forwards and slipped one hand up Amelia's naked thigh and under her skirt, cupping her buttock and then patting it. "Good girl! Kept the skirt up and left another mark?" he asked.

"As if I wouldn't....and you know I did!" Amelia replied, smiling.

"Go and get changed then, and put your collar on! You know I hate seeing you without it," Brian told her.

Amelia stood up and let go of the breast she had been squeezing and mauling and turned to go. A whip hissed and smacked further along the arena and she saw that Tony had got another of the slaves tied out in full X shaped extension inside a tall rectangular frame and was starting to wield a single tail whip across her back. The slave's feet were held clear of the ground so the body was spectacularly stretched. As she watched a second lash smacked home and Amelia's heart leaped in excitement at the sight of the slave's breasts wobbling as her body shook. She recognised her as being one of the longest serving ones; Cherry. She took her name from the spectacular shade her nipples turned with arousal and as the third and fourth lashes landed they blossomed forth. Amelia went across and reached up to tweak them as the whipping continued. The slave's head was thrown back and languidly it rolled forwards in response to this new stimulation. Amelia saw her face was calm and relaxed, her eyes were bright and alert though and Amelia got the feeling that the whipping might not be as much of a punishment as Tony meant it to be. She had had a hard day's training by the look of her, she was scratched and dirty and had clearly been under the lash plenty of times already that day. It was unusual for Cherry to be punished because she was one of the most biddable and hard working of the slaves – she was never going to be star material but she could be relied on to run, fight and compete until she dropped.

Tony looked out from behind her.

"She's been a right cow today," he told her as if he had been reading her thoughts. "I reckon she needs playing with for a night. Check her records when you get in will you? And can you take Legs and Tigre when you go? This one needs a good thrashing so I'll be here for a while."

Amelia bit her lip with excitement; this was what she so missed, the mastery so complete that only the slave's body was there at all. The rest of her was simply an irrelevance. They were their owners' creations, superb animals for providing pleasure in whatever ways their masters required.

Over at the far edge of the arena two more slaves stood with placid patience, they were tethered by slender leather leashes that ran from their heavy tongue rings to more rings set in the top of the boarding. Their hands were clipped together behind their backs. Occasionally they would shift their weight from one leg to the other or swallow saliva and champ on their rings and the leash's karabiner.

As they had finished for the day and the weather was cold, either Brian or Tony had slipped thick 'poncho' type blankets over their heads and belted them around their waists. Amelia went up to them and patted their haunches and stroked their hair. With Legs she had to stretch up a little, the tall slave lived up to her nickname and was used primarily in dressage and short distance pony races. Beside her was another of the old lags, the gypsy girl, Tigre, dark and fierce, a committed masochist who would only tolerate being handled by women if she knew a man wasn't far away. However Brian had often let Amelia hone her whip skills on Tigre's lithe form and the dark eyes were respectful rather than hostile. Amelia slid her hand under the blanket and teased the slave's clitoris for a few seconds, just as a hello, then she gathered the leashes and led them off, clicking her tongue and picking up her case as she went. She put the leashes over one shoulder and negotiated the small door at the far end of the arena then set off along the short path that led to the CSL yard. The slaves were housed in a long, low block on the right and above them the grooms had their quarters.

Amelia pushed open the door and led her charges in, dropped her case and then tethered them to rings set in the wall behind the door and looked around. A chorus of greetings came from the other grooms, Raika, Anna Marie, Eve and Helga. The head groom herself, Patti Campbell was bending down examining a slave's foot, which she was holding up behind her.

"Hi, Amelia!" she called. "Help get those two sluiced down and stabled will you? Blackie here's gone lame and I'll have to get Dr Sands down to check her out."

Amelia took a moment to drink in the atmosphere of her final destination. The grooms all had their uniforms – which she would change into shortly – of kitten heeled sandals and short kilt worn below a blouse knotted beneath the breasts – they were busy putting the slaves through the end of day sluicing prior to serving them their evening feed. Along the ceiling ran an adapted warehouse system of frames slung beneath rails, Helga stood by the showers and controlled the progress of the naked and spreadeagled bodies - once Raika had chained them - as they were passed through the steaming showers and Anna Marie worked the long handled sponge into all the necessary nooks and crannies. Once they were washed and dried by being passed between powerful hot air blowers, Eve took them down and chained them back in their stalls.

And while the other girls served the food and made sure the bottle in each stall was topped up with the mixture of fruit juice and chilled sperm that Patti swore by, Amelia took her case upstairs and changed into her uniform, fastening her beloved collar around her neck in the little room with its dormer window overlooking the parkland, its luxurious en suite shower room and comfortable bed. Her master's apartment was on the opposite side of the yard which the CSL buildings were grouped round and as yet she didn't know whether he would want her in her own bed or his. But there was time enough to worry about that.

She ate her supper with the other girls in the new dining room that now opened off Patti's office and which led onto the new kitchen, thus saving the girls the chore of having to collect food from the main kitchens. Alberto, the chef, had prepared his usual superb meal for the staff after having catered for the slaves' individual diets. He came out while they were cleaning their plates of the very last traces of profiteroles and Patti suggested he take Cherry into the dungeon for an evening's play – Tony having brought her and Fiji back while Amelia was changing – a quick riffle through Cherry's records had shown that she hadn't been used for a few weeks and was probably in need of serious attention. It was most likely the cause of her uncharacteristic bad behaviour.

The rumour amongst the staff was that Alberto had upset one wife and several mistresses too many and that John Carpenter, The Lodge's owner, had offered him a hideout with a perpetual supply of women in return for his catering for the arena slaves and their grooms. Grinning broadly he strode out into the stall area and they heard him leading Cherry out.

"Hey! She been whipped good already!" he called.

"You want me to come and show you some more places you can whip her?" Patti called back.

"No! Just show me where I can whip *you!*" he laughed and they heard him encourage Cherry into the dungeon at the far end of the stalls.

The grooms smiled as well as Patti poured them some more wine.

"He gave me such a leathering with the crop last week!" Patti admitted. "But he's pretty good with his cock as well," she added.

Amelia spotted Raika, the pretty, petite Indian groom, looking out anxiously into the office and the stables beyond and she smiled quietly. No change there then! Patti had called Chrissie Sands, the house doctor up at The Lodge and the CSL stable's vet, down to check on Blackie. Apart from her professional duties, she was also Raika's adored Mistress. They heard the door to the yard open and before it closed Raika was out of her seat and greeting the slender doctor.

"Besotted!" Patti said, rolling her eyes. Amelia detected the familiar trace of jealousy in the Scotswoman's voice, all the grooms loved having Raika in their beds, she was always desperate to please and could give some of the best cunnilingus any of them had ever had. But with the coming of Dr Sands, Raika rarely spent her nights at the stable. And when she did, her heart wasn't in it. However, as head groom, Patti still held sway over her and frequently concocted an excuse to whip the superb body and enjoy the subsequent gratitude of the penitent.

But in the complicated entanglement of SM relationships within the CSL/ Lodge set up, Chrissie Sands, who out-ranked Patti, often found an excuse to put Patti herself on the whipping post and thus enjoy the rewards of administering discipline.

Patti got up from the table and went to join the doctor and the three remaining girls caught up on months of gossip. Were there going to be any new additions to the complement of slaves, were there any new diabolically cruel twists to the contests in the arenas? Were there any new Housegirls? When were the slaves next going to be rented out to other stables for an event? And most importantly, were there any new and maybe crueller Masters at The Lodge

After a satisfactory, and much needed, gossip which confirmed that indeed most of the slaves would be hired out very shortly, Amelia decided to go and see what was happening with Blackie. The slave was laid out on the examination table, her wrists still cuffed together but her legs raised and spread on stirrups. The doctor was manipulating and massaging an area around one of Blackie's ankles. The slave occasionally emitted gasps of discomfort.

"Strain. Nothing more," Chrissie Sands opined at last. Everything about her was clipped and precise and self assured. "Leave her in her stall for a week and then light – and tell Carlo I mean *light* - training for a week and then I'll take another look at her."

The women giggled as moans began to come from the open door of the dungeon. It was Cherry heading for one of her noisy orgasms and she was joined by Alberto's hoarser groans until they both reached a climax and there was silence. A few seconds later Alberto appeared, doing up his flies.

"I tell Helga to take her down," he said and disappeared off to his apartment, from where he would probably ring for a Housegirl, his appetites were insatiable. Raika took Blackie back to her stall and then trotted after the doctor up to the house.

Patti Campbell tossed back her spectacular copper coloured hair and gave Amelia a thoughtful look.

"Your boss won't be back for a while yet. He'll have a dram or two in the Common Room. Helga's on duty down here, so do you fancy a quick one?"

Amelia let her eyes run over the woman's lush curves, her blouse straining to contain the magnificent breasts, her long, pale and smooth thighs showing above her trademark, black suede, thigh boots.

"In the dungeon?" she asked.

Patti laughed and led the way into the room, closing the door behind her. It was a long room with heavy blinds on the windows and a deep piled, blood red carpet on the floor. The walls and ceiling were padded as well so that Lodge members – or the male CSL staff – could enjoy any slave or groom they wanted without disturbing anyone else. Alternatively during summer the windows could be opened so that everyone could enjoy the groans and screams.

The only other occupant as the women entered was spectacularly displayed on an X frame. Cherry had been fastened to it face out and after her beating it had been tipped back horizontally on its axis so that Alberto had been able to enter her easily and conveniently. Without needing to say anything, both Amelia and Patti approached the motionless figure, the slave's head hung back between her outstretched arms but as she heard them she craned it up and they saw a look of exhausted contentment on her face. Alberto had not let her earlier thrashing stand in the way of his enjoyment and Cherry's nipples jutted, hard and deepest cheery red, from the peaks of breasts that carried a criss-crossing lattice of pink stripes. Her stomach had also been dealt with and her inner thighs and her cunt had received special attention. The handle of the flogger that had done the damage was rammed into the cunt and its leather tails trailed down towards the floor.

Amelia ran her hands over the flogged skin, feeling the slight raising of the abrasions on the warm, velvet smooth texture of breasts and thighs. Cherry's stomach fluttered and heaved as she began to pant almost immediately in the face of renewed attention. Patti gently rubbed a fingertip over the exposed clitoris.

It always fascinated Amelia how the arena stables produced such athletic creatures that nevertheless retained their soft femininity. Even in extension, Cherry kept her feminine curves and her powerful thighs were smooth and graceful. Suddenly she felt an urgent need to orgasm. Before, she had just felt mildly excited at the prospect of sex with Patti, but now she knew she had to enjoy this slave. Patti obviously felt the same.

"Aren't they lovely after a good beating?" she said.

Amelia's throat was dry and her voice failed her so she simply nodded.

"But I suppose we all are!" Patti laughed and went quickly to a shelf, stripped to just her boots and took a strap-on down. Amelia watched her with mounting lust. Her skin had the almost translucent pallor of some red heads and was firm and smooth despite the lush contours. With no trace of self-consciousness she parted her legs widely and fed the dildo's straps between them then fastened them tightly and came back to Amelia with the long black shaft wagging in front of her. Her breasts swung and shifted as she walked and Amelia shed her blouse and skirt with fumbling haste, then eagerly bent over between Cherry's tied open legs, tugging the whip free of the moist embrace of the vagina.

She let her mouth and nose hover over the slave's still open, flogged and seeping cunt, savouring the odours of male and female emissions that glistened at its entrance and made shiny snail trails down and across the thighs and the buttock crease.

Slowly she let her tongue stray over Cherry's smooth skin, licking and flicking, from right thigh to left, fetching sighs of pleasure from the slave. Behind her Patti's fingers strayed over her own buttocks and then found their way easily into her own vagina as her own tongue found its way into Cherry and sampled the rich blend of tastes as the fluids trickled out and oozed, thick and oily across her tongue. The slave's soft inner tissues caressed Amelia's tongue as it quested more deeply into the juice soaked tunnel. Her face was bathed in the dampness of the recent fuck and she gloried in it as Patti's strap-on finally barged into her own, flooding sheath. For a further few moments, Amelia stayed where she was, legs splayed, and bent over between's Cherry's widespread legs, letting Patti settle into a rhythm inside her and enjoying the feel of the thick slime running down her cheeks.

But as Patti's thrusts became more demanding, she moved up the slave's body until her face was over the rounded pillows of breastflesh with their spectacular crowns of deep red nipples. With her pelvis now braced firmly against Cherry's, Amelia was able to withstand the hard, pounding thrusts that Patti was making, and cramming her mouth full of one nipple and areola and clawing her hand over the other, she began to nip and pinch at Cherry's already punished tits. The slave's head jerked up and she made incoherent moans – it didn't matter whether they were of protest or pleasure, apart from her body, the slave was an irrelevance – and Amelia bit harder, loving the feel of the rubbery tube between her teeth.

Patti began to really fuck in earnest and Amelia heard her gasp as the clit rasper on the dildo had its inevitable effect. Amelia raised herself and then sank down to rasp her own clit against the slave's pubic bone and succeeded in starting her own spiral upwards towards orgasm. She clawed deeper into one breast and bit harder on the other as Patti remorselessly hammered home the rubber shaft of the strap-on. Below her, she felt Cherry's stomach begin to flutter and her hips try and thrust up at her and briefly, just as the firework show started, she felt a stab of deepest pleasure at the thought that the slave would be denied a climax. It was that thought that plunged her over the edge and into the maelstrom of orgasm as Patti finally stopped fucking her and collapsed heavily onto her back. For a moment they lay, cushioned on the forlornly begging slave's body – its hips just twitching hopefully.

Gradually Amelia became aware that someone was standing beside the tableau and blearily she looked up. It was Helga and she was holding Amelia's mobile phone which she had left in her bag in the dining room.

"Your Master rang for you about five minutes ago but I couldn't find you. He said he wanted you to come immediately." She grinned broadly. "I don't think this is what he meant though!"

Swearing under her breath and still re-tying her blouse up under her breasts, Amelia stumbled out into the cold night air. He would have to ring while she was having a shag! He was always in urgent need of one himself after he'd been up at the house for an evening and now he was going to go ape with her for not being where a good slave should be; exactly where her master needed her.

Under her kilt she still felt warm and dilated, her nipples chafed at the blouse with the cold re-erecting them. She hastily finger-combed her hair, scurried to the door of her master's apartment and entered.

He was in the kitchen, pouring himself a liqueur.

"I'm sorry I wasn't there when you rang, Sir," she began and then paused, toying with the idea of making some excuse, but then realised that the thought of punishment was deeply appealing just now. "Patti was shagging me in the dungeon," she said simply.

Brian cocked his head in the direction of his lounge, where an exposed beam provided convenient hanging space for a slave.

"Get your kit off and your restraints on," he told her curtly and drained his glass.

Her heart singing at the prospect of pain, Amelia undressed for the third time that evening and buckled on her ankle and wrist restraints that were kept in the top drawer of a sideboard. Obediently she held her hands up and apart for Brian to fasten the karabiners on the cuffs to the rings in the beam. He came to stand behind her and ran his hands over her body proprietorially. She shivered deliciously as she felt them slide over her hips and sweep across her buttocks, then run up her back and round, under her arms to re-acquaint themselves with her breasts. And her nipples. He kissed her neck as he took a firm grip on both of them and pinched and twisted simultaneously. Amelia gasped as the pain triggered the fires in her belly again and she longed for her master to take complete control of her and punish her if it pleased him to.

He tormented the tight little nubs several more times before he made her sigh by letting them go and plunging his hands down to her groin and pinching her clitoris between the sides of his hands as he slid them between her legs, cupping her cunt but not making any attempt to enter it. Amelia whimpered her need and made him laugh. He stood back and then left her to go upstairs. She heard his heavy footsteps as he moved around the bedroom and she knew he was selecting a whip to use on her – and maybe something more. She shivered in excited anticipation of clamps, pegs or maybe even needles – it had been ages since she'd had them!

When he came back down he pulled her ankles apart and shackled them to chains running from rings set low in the walls on either side of the lounge. Amelia relished the sense of captivity and helplessness that the increased strain on her arms gave her. And of course it meant that her legs were open and her cunt was exposed. She craned her head round to watch Brian shake out a single tail whip and position himself a little way off and to her side.

Then he whipped her and for Amelia the night turned into a scarlet display of delight as a series of stinging, hot lashes seared across her back and wrapped her ribs; biting cruelly at the side of her breast. She counted twenty before she became unable to frame the numbers, even in her mind and instead yielded her being entirely to her master and to his whip.

Eventually the lashes stopped and Amelia hung exhausted from her wrists. Her whole body burned and stung in a way she loved so much that she would sometimes wake up in her London flat and be distraught when she realised that she had only been dreaming that Brian was lashing her harder and more cruelly than he had ever done before – harder even than he beat the arena slaves. He took her down without saying a word and clicked his fingers. She dropped onto all fours and crawled upstairs after him, smiling a secret little smile as she savoured the whip burn.

She crouched, naked, by the bed and watched him undress, her eyes devouring the play of muscles beneath his skin.

At last he came to stand over her, now naked himself, his imperious cock swollen and hard, rearing above her.

He made a slight beckoning gesture and she rose up onto her knees and took him gently and respectfully between her lips. As she had known he would he tasted richly of other women and she derived deep satisfaction from knowing that at the end of the day, hers was the mouth he chose to grace. He didn't finish there though, deciding instead to take her in his bed.

Amelia's day ended precisely as she would have wished, her master's weight drove her down into the mattress as he rammed himself towards his pleasure inside her cunt. His majestic shaft spread her labia and her tunnel to their widest and every inch was stimulated by his strong, dominating thrusts as they increased in fervour. She held on desperately against her own climax as she felt him reach a ferocious peak and then she heard him gasp as he held himself hard against the neck of her womb, his fingers tightened their hold on her whipped bottom and she allowed herself to come as he spent himself.

Before she fell into a deep sleep with her master's arm draped across her shoulders and his body pressed close against her back, Amelia told herself she felt utterly complete and just for a moment the previous weeks' doubts dissipated.

CHAPTER 2.

"What the hell do I want to come to a strip club for?" Diane asked in horrified amazement as the doorman opened the heavy door at the foot of the stairs that had led down from the shabby Soho street, and she peered inside to see the almost nude girl whirling and posing on the catwalk above the audience's heads.

Geoff looked around and gave her his infuriating, casual grin. "It'll be fun, Babe. C'mon, I often come here!"

It was the first she had heard of it and Diane felt a dull ache of unease in her stomach, Geoff had been behaving oddly these last few days. Almost trying to quarrel with her, as if he was pushing her away. This evening though, he had promised would be one she wouldn't forget, it would make up for things, he said, but even as she had excitedly envisaged candlelit restaurants, she had noticed a harsh gleam in his eye that she had never noticed before.

Now Geoff winked at the doorman and sauntered in leaving Diane to either turn tail, strike up a relationship with the hulking man or follow him in.

She followed him and was immediately subjected to openly appraising stares from all sides, as if just being in the place meant she was a stripper too. Instinctively she clasped her jacket closed across her breasts and hurried after Geoff who had found a table.

"Just look at the knockers on that!" he said as she joined him. Just above the table, on the catwalk that ran from the stage to the end wall of the club a redhead wearing just a thong was rubbing her breasts together and pouting at the audience in what she clearly thought was a provocative manner.

"Jeez, I'd like to shoot my load between those!" he said.

Diane was shocked and bewildered. Geoff had never behaved like this before. She had never seen him so blatantly crude and lascivious – not to mention so bloody male fascist! He waved a waitress over and put his arm round her waist while he ordered – and presumed to order for her too! She just gaped at him as the waitress smiled and presented her bottom, under a short, maid's skirt to be patted before she trotted away.

"I like this place!" he said, leaning back in his seat, obviously quite comfortable, even as the girl on the catwalk bent forward, facing away from them and presented them with a no-holds-barred view of her shapely bottom and long thighs, her plump genitals only hidden by a stretched, scarlet scrap of lace. But not for long, Diane thought grimly. Instinctively she began to compare herself with the girl Geoff was now staring up at hungrily.

She could match the length of leg and the bottom. Her breasts weren't far off either. She couldn't match the girl's big red hair but wouldn't want to. Brunette was fine with her. But what she *really* couldn't match was the shameless way the girl was displaying herself. She would never be able to do that and Geoff seemed to be enjoying it so much!

"When you move in, Babe, we'll be able to come down here lots!"

The drinks arrived and Diane hurriedly took a swig of lukewarm lager. She had sold her flat to move in with this guy who was suddenly behaving like a chauvinistic throwback.

Well she might just have to buy another flat, she wasn't standing for this any longer.

"Call me a cab. I'm leaving," she said flatly, slamming her drink down decisively.

Geoff shrugged and took a long slug of his drink. "You're a cab. Bye, Diane."

She gaped at him. Shocked beyond belief. It was as though he had engineered this evening out deliberately to dump her in the most brutal fashion. In just seconds he had wiped out two years. Eyes blurring with tears, Diane stood up and hurried towards the door.

The doorman took one look at her and reached for his mobile phone.

"I'll call a taxi," he told her and she nodded gratefully, surreptitiously wiping her nose and eyes with a hankie while he spoke into the phone. "Wait at the top of the stairs, he'll be there in a minute," he told her.

Diane waited in the recessed doorway, breathing in the damp night air and trying to think coolly. What had come over Geoff? He wasn't like that! Not a bit like that! He'd been kind and funny and a wonderful lover. He had known how to pleasure a woman with his tongue better than any man she had ever known. He had lain for what seemed like hours between her wide-spread thighs, licking and penetrating her with his tongue, then kissing his way up the inside of each long thigh until she was quivering and begging him to lick her all over again.

She shivered with excitement at the memory, even as a fresh burst of tears clouded her eyes. But then a London cab pulled up in a clatter of diesel and she trotted out into the drizzle. Another fare was just exiting the cab and he held the door open for her as she clambered in gratefully.

But then suddenly the man had turned and was climbing in straight after her.

"What??" she squeaked. "This is my....Hey! Driver!" The man put a hand over her mouth as the door slammed and the cab moved off. Then his weight pinned her down and his other hand moved to her arm. She felt a sharp pricking sensation and he moved off her. Too stunned for words she looked down at the hypodermic syringe being emptied into her wrist and looked up at the man's grim, set face.

"Why?" she managed before the world seemed to get smaller and then just turn off.

She came round briefly to find herself lying on some sort of hard table or trolley. The room didn't look like a hospital though, it looked more like a cellar somewhere, but with bright lights. Somehow it all seemed very distant and unimportant. A tall man in a white coat stood over her with some sort of clipboard, he was reading from it and glancing down at her.

"Sold up and about to move into her boss's flat. Moving away from her friends.....fell out with mother ten years ago. She doesn't trust her Stepdad. Perfect! Not many going to worry about you, are they Diane?"

She tried to make some kind of noise in agreement, it all seemed quite reasonable. But then he smiled and leaned down closer.

"You're going back to sleep for a while and when you wake you'll be in a very different place. You're going on a long journey, won't that be nice?"

She tried to nod, a long journey sounded very nice; she couldn't quite remember why, but she recalled being very upset and unhappy about something. A long journey would be perfect. Just what the doctor ordered.

She went under again.

The next time she regained consciousness her mouth was dry and her eyes sticky. She blinked and licked her lips then tried to move. Her arms were piniomed behind her and she could feel ties at her wrists when she tried to move. Her head began to clear and she took in a rough cinderblock wall in front of her face, the feel of coarse blankets under her. She turned her head as much as she could and saw a naked light bulb hanging in front of what looked like the barred door of a prison cell. A man was standing on the other side of it and as Diane struggled with sudden urgency to turn over and sit up, he retreated and she heard him call out something in a language she didn't understand.

Panting with effort and panic, she made it to a sitting position on the edge of a narrow bed in what was now clearly revealed to be a cell with rough walls, a toilet and a sink. Her ankles weren't bound and she tottered upright then staggered as the last of whatever they had given her made the room spin. Then she tried to yell and found her voice came out as just a pathetic croak. She coughed and spluttered for a moment and then tried again.

She called for help, her voice stronger but still more shrill than normal, and immediately she heard other female voices raised in similar cries. She pressed her face against the bars.

"What's going on!? Where am I? Get me out of here! Get the British Consul!" she screamed, it was all she could think of.

The room in which the cells were set was a long, low-ceilinged one with its far wall about ten feet away from the cell doors. The man Diane had seen had vanished but now a door in the far wall opened and a woman walked in.

She turned on a much stronger light which only illuminated the grime and dirt on the walls but at least it illuminated her as well. She was dressed in a smart, grey, skirt suit and was tall, maybe five foot ten. But as Diane's shouts began to die away in the face of the woman's calm smile, she realised that she was shapely as well; long, strong, nylon-clad legs disappeared under the skirt which started a couple of inches above the knee and strained tightly across powerful thighs. A simple white shirt covered her flat stomach and then swelled out spectacularly over her breasts. The top three buttons were undone and even from this distance, Diane could see the valley of the cleavage begin. Her strong face was framed by honey blonde hair that cascaded onto her shoulders.

Diane realised the cell she was in was on the extreme left of the line of cells, and away to her right other occupants were also beginning to realise their yelling was having no effect at all. Slowly silence descended.

When she was certain she had the prisoners' full attention, the woman walked forwards slowly, her high heels clicking on the concrete floor.

"Good day, Ladies. I'm afraid I have bad news for you," she said, standing about five feet in front of the centre of the line of cells and turning to right and left slightly as she spoke to all the occupants. "You've been abducted and are destined to spend the rest of your lives as slaves. What the more lurid press call sex-slaves in fact."

She smiled her calm smile and clasped her hands behind her as the import of her words sank in. Then the yelling and screaming began again from some of the cells.

Diane didn't yell this time. Her mind was fully alert now and she was recalling how Geoff had been behaving in the days before that weird night at the strip club – almost deliberately pushing her away. The bastard! The complete and utter, snivelling, treacherous bastard! He had been waiting for her to sell her flat and then he and whoever-they-were had engineered that night deliberately to provoke her into leaving by carefully prepared cab. How much had he got for her? The bastard had actually sold her! *Her!* Not just another human being, but his own bloody girlfriend!

A forlorn hope emerged from the fog of fury in her mind.

"Look, I've got some money! Just let me out and I'll pay you. Honestly! I've just sold a flat in London, I can pay you well to let me go! Please!"

The woman again rode the storms of similar protests that arose from the other cells.

"I'm sorry but the answer to all of you is, no! None of you has enough money to make it worth ransoming you – believe me I know! You have been sold by boyfriends, husbands, girlfriends – and in two cases Mistresses. We will train you and sell you on."

Diane broke into tears and sank to her knees as the woman went on remorselessly.

"You have been brought into Eastern Europe. While all the authorities are looking for girls being trafficked West, we find it best to go East instead. There is nowhere for you to escape to and we've never lost a girl yet in any case. So please do put thoughts of escape from your heads, they will only slow your progress towards your true destiny. Your profiles all suggest that you will take to slavery quite easily, but our job is to leave nothing to chance. By the time you leave us, you will be fully resigned to a life of submission to the pleasure of others. Later on you will probably come to enjoy it, but by then it will be irrelevant, slavery will be the only life you know."

The woman paused and walked up and down the line of cells. Diane sniffed and tried to stop her sobs as the woman came to stand in front of her. She looked up piteously into a stony gaze from icy blue eyes before the woman moved on. From the other cells came the sounds of females crying brokenly. Resuming her place in the centre of the room the woman went on.

"Get it all out, Ladies, and then we'll get down to work. The sooner we get started the sooner you will realise that there is no going back."

For a moment the wailing increased and then died into silence again.

"My name is Doctor Williams but you will call me Madam," the woman went on. "Now I expect you're all hungry as you've been out for well over twenty-four hours."

Diane discovered to her amazement that she was.

"Stand with your backs to the doors of your cells and push your wrists between the bars."

As Diane did so she saw the main door open again and a man enter, in a few moments she felt a blade saw through what must have been plastic ties and then she was free. She rubbed her wrists although they weren't that sore and took stock again. She was still dressed in the trousers she had been wearing, although they looked pretty creased now. Her sweater was getting a bit itchy and her knickers felt hot and uncomfortable. How had they been transported, she wondered. Train, plane? How many girls were there? And did the woman mean they were meant for some Godforsaken hellhole of a brothel? If that was it, she would kill herself rather than submit.

The door in the far wall opened again and, looking a little bizarre under the circumstances, a food trolley was wheeled in by another woman. As she started ladling food onto plates, Diane wondered about the possibility of appealing to some sisterly feeling and maybe getting help from her. But Doctor Williams nipped that thought in the bud.

She strode across and grasped the woman's hair in her fist, dragging her head up.

"This sorry excuse for a slut belongs to me, heart and soul! So don't even think of trying to corrupt her. She lives to be beaten by me! I own her, understand? She was once just like you. So look well at what your future holds, you'll be just as much a slave as she is!"

The Doctor smiled down at the grimacing woman and planted a kiss on her lips, lightly. The woman smiled back and went back to serving food.

"Stand at the backs of your cells!" the Doctor ordered.

The Doctor's slave who turned out to be a rather voluptuous black haired beauty, dressed only in a short white coat, pushed shallow bowls of broth under the bars with slabs of bread to go with it.

Surprisingly, it was extremely good and Diane wolfed hers down sitting on the edge of the bed. It occurred to her that if she was so totally in their power that these people could do anything with her, then the fact that they chose to feed her well might mean she had real value to them. In which case the rest of the treatment mightn't be so bad and she could play along until a chance to escape came up.

Once the meal was over they were made to stick their wrists through the bars again to have them bound and then they were let out. Diane reckoned there were about ten females but Doctor Williams now had several very large men standing against the wall and they held coiled whips in their hands.

The women were herded through the door and out into a huge, semi-derelict sort of warehouse, Diane thought, and here they were made to line up with the men behind them. Far above them a corrugated asbestos roof with some glazed panels let in pale daylight which illuminated a huge space littered with odd bits of derelict machinery. Chains hung from massive iron beams here and there. In contrast to the rusting iron there were also brand new, sinister frames and posts the like of which Diane had never seen before, but which nevertheless started a shiver of unease in her.

The Doctor stood with a pile of clothes of some sort in front of her while the girls looked around them. There was a door over on the far right, it looked as if it was only made of tin. Diane glanced across at her neighbour, a nervous, slender blonde and the two exchanged the slightest of nods; they were both thinking the same thing.

"Now these gentlemen behind you, who you're going to get know really well in the coming weeks, are going to cut your wrists free again and then you're going to strip and put on your new uniforms."

Diane and her neighbour exchanged looks again. It had to be worth a try. Diane felt her ties being cut again and as soon as they had gone she bolted at the same time as every other girl who had been freed. Filling the huge space with their echoing cries they charged for the door they had all seen. It wobbled open as the first girl fell against it and shrieking, the rest poured through after her. They emerged into a brand new, fully secured yard with rolls of razor wire on top of smoothly rendered walls, fully fifteen feet high. There was no gate. Diane looked around in desperation and then cupped her hands and screamed for help.

Doctor Williams and the men strolled through the door.

"Feel free," she told Diane. "There's no one for miles. Now back into line and let's get on!"

The girls slumped and shuffled into line when they were ordered and then made a half hearted attempt to march back inside. Diane couldn't be bothered to try and keep in step. She was furious and ashamed at how easily they had been fooled – and how effective a tactic it had been – she had to admit. Far better to let them try and escape and fail miserably than merely tell them not to.

"Now strip and put on these!" the Doctor ordered when they had stumbled back into a ragged and sniffling line. She held up something that was not much more than a shirt that buttoned down the front.

Four men were carrying out a padded bench, a little like a vaulting horse as she spoke and Diane felt that discretion was the better part of valour.

The only problem was that there were men standing behind her. She half turned to ascertain that that was still the case and sure enough a leering fair haired man was leaning against the wall behind her and more men seemed to have entered until there were as many men as girls, and they all had whips.

Diane's heart sank; she had a bad feeling that this nightmarish day was about to get worse.

But there was really nothing she could do except pull her sweater off and throw it down before reaching behind her and undoing her bra. She risked a glance along the line and saw a row of bobbing breasts, two pairs of much darker ones, she noted, as girls shed their bras and began to unzip skirts, trousers and jeans. It would be quite a view from behind, she reflected as she pushed her trousers down and stamped her feet to get them off, then closed her eyes as she hooked her thumbs into her knickers' side straps and went for it; the full bend forwards and step out. The man behind her was getting a perfect view of what she had been looking at in the strip club, she thought bitterly. But there was just a touch of pride in the thought that what she had was a match for that redheaded tart.

"I'll give you all a full examination in the morning," the Doctor told them as she went along the line, handing out the shirts and a pair of plain plastic flip-flops to each girl. Diane gratefully buttoned herself into hers and shuffled her feet into the shoes, but found the buttons didn't start anywhere near high enough to prevent a good couple of inches of cleavage being plainly on view. And the hem was only at about mid thigh at front and rear with an upward curve in between to expose more at the sides. The garments were worn, and had faded grey and green stripes on them, but they were plainly designed to make each girl almost as available as if she were naked. Diane looked along the line and had to admit that some of the girls didn't look at all bad. She hated bitches who could wear bin liners and still look good! She stopped herself suddenly. Hadn't that been why Sandy, her erstwhile best friend, had got fed up with being seen round with her? She looked down and had to admit the long smooth thighs beneath the shirt did look quite sexy.

"Now we will start your discipline," the Doctor said and Diane's thoughts were instantly derailed. "You will not be surprised to learn that we frown on escape attempts. And seeing as pretty well all of you tried, we might as well punish all of you." She gestured at the padded bench. "It'll take some time but that's alright, I wasn't planning on doing much tonight anyway." She gave the girls a humourless smile.

From the far right of the line a girl was pushed forwards by a tall man. She stumbled and then tried to scramble back, to escape, to do anything other than walk towards that sinister bench.

The man was implacable however and eventually he grabbed her by her arm and marched her the last few yards. She was powerless to prevent herself being flung face down across the padded top and held there while other men crouched and tied her frantically kicking feet to each of the legs. Then her hands were dealt with and finally the tail of her shirt was flicked up over her back and the cane appeared. The doctor's slave crept up to her mistress and handed it to her with what was almost reverence. Nine horrified pairs of eyes followed the wickedly slender shaft as the Doctor sliced the air with it and regarded the shapely and trembling buttocks before her with blatant lust.

Diane had never seen a girl so totally exposed as this wretched one was. Where the girl in the strip club had had a gently bulging purse of lace to contain her labia, here the cunt was naked and vulnerable in its hollow between the tops of the thighs, a dark fringe of pubic hair was all that protected it. The girl's back could be seen shaking with sobs as the cane whistled through the air behind her.

Then the Doctor laid the shaft across the trembling buttocks and settled her feet. Diane watched in terror as the Doctor's hand lifted away and then there was a brief zipping sound and the flesh of the buttocks was rippling in the aftermath of the strike. The huge room they stood in echoed instantly to the shriek from the girl, whose head snapped up in agony.

Before anyone could react the Doctor had swung in another lash and the victim choked on her cry as she hadn't finished screaming from the first. Two strangely double lines now tracked across the hitherto smooth expanse of flesh.

"These are called tramlines," the Doctor explained, tracing them with the tip of the cane and making the girl wince. "You'll become familiar with them soon enough. By the time we've finished tonight you'll all have ten of 'em to start with!"

As her words sank in she went back to work and swished in four more lashes in quick succession, fetching frenzied howls and shrieks from her victim whose writhing at her bonds became so desperate that the Doctor stopped the beating temporarily. She bent forwards and grabbed a fistful of hair, as she had with her slave.

"You know damn well you've had the cane before..... Annie isn't it?"

For a moment victim and tormentor stayed quite still, staring at each other.

Then the Doctor shook her impatiently. "Well!!!??" she bellowed. "You've been caned before haven't you, you little bitch? Answer me!"

Slowly the beaten girl nodded, was let go and collapsed, sobbing.

The Doctor turned to her captive audience. "You see there's no point in trying to fool us. This little slut was sold to us by her Mistress who told us she was trained to the cane. I know which of you will find this a life changing experience and which of you won't. So let's not waste time."

With no warning the woman spun on her heel and lashed in the final blows of the sentence in a relentless avalanche of agony. This time however, the girl did no more than fidget her feet and bounce on her toes.

Then she was released and taken back to her cell. Diane was astonished to see that she was dry eyed as she was taken away, although she was biting her lower lip.

The Doctor whacked her way through four more sentences before she handed over the cane to her slave. As she told them, there was no reason why the later victims should take any softer lashes than the earlier ones, and if anyone thought a slave would go easier on her sisters, then Livia would prove them wrong. And Diane watched in gathering dismay as the slave; Livia, tucked her long black hair back, undid two buttons on her coat and slammed in a beating as harsh as anything her mistress had doled out. The sixth quivering, scored bottom was covered and its owner led away and still the punishments went on. The blonde next to Diane took her beating with surprising fortitude and she witnessed an odd, secretive smile pass between the slave and the blonde as she straightened up from her punishment.

But then it was Diane's turn. There was no point in struggling, that had been tried before; instead she squared her shoulders and strode forward as firmly as her quivering insides and legs would allow her. She tried to stand and stare into the distance impassively, scorning their attempts to cow her, head held high, as her legs were spread and her ankles shackled to the feet of the bench.

The Doctor strolled across as the men finished and stood back. She took hold of Diane's face and turned it towards her. Diane stared into the woman's blue eyes and noted the cruel smile just twitching the corners of her full-lipped mouth upwards.

"Livia!" the Doctor called without taking her eyes off Diane. "This one thinks she's ever so superior and refuses to show fear. She imagines she has dignity and can overcome our squalid games by regal disdain. But she has never felt the cane! Strip her of her pride, Livia, or I'll have you hanging by your wrists all night!"

"Yes, Mistress! Shall I give her just the ten?"

There was a pause and Diane felt her lower lip begin to tremble at the thought of even more punishment, despite all her efforts to restrain it and keep her eyes locked with those of the sadistic bitch in front of her. The woman laughed as she saw the movement.

"Give her ten – to start with. And strip her first."

Roughly the woman pushed her away and before she could protest, her shirt was ripped down the front and pulled from her, then a hand shoved her hard in the back and she was propelled down onto the sweat sodden padding of the bench, her breasts crushed beneath her. Two men stepped forwards and tied her hands to the bench legs. Fortunately her hair fell thickly over her face and she was unable to see the contemptuous leers they would doubtless be giving her.

But her relief was short lived. The Doctor squatted down in front of her and pulled her hair back, making it plain she was going to live every jot of the suffering that was coming Diane's way.

The cane tapped gently across her buttocks, was lifted away, came back and tapped again.....was lifted away again........the Doctor grinned openly as Diane's face crinkled into a grimace of despair. Inwardly she was shrieking at the wretched slave to get on with the punishment and the Doctor knew it.

Then the first lash caught her. Whether Livia had really laid it on in fear of her Mistress' wrath or whether it was because it was her first cane stroke, the agony was appalling after the initial second's numbness. With her head held up, her throat was stretched and so her cry was weak. After a second scorching lash, it was stronger.

"That's better!" the Doctor said. "I like to hear a slave sing!"

Whack!

Whack!

Whack!

Livia, despite being a slave herself, beat out a relentless tattoo of pain on Diane's helpless body while she entertained the Doctor by screaming until her throat was raw.

They gave her a rest for a few moments at the halfway stage and she took the second half of her punishment behind the curtain of her hair. Snot and tears running down her face as she drowned helplessly in the pain she couldn't avoid. By the final lash she was no longer feeling the individual strikes. There was just an all enveloping sensation that had soared far beyond any pain Diane had ever known.

She didn't stop snivelling even when the lashes stopped. Eventually her hair was pulled up again and the Doctor's smiling face was in front of her tear-blurred eyes.

"Now, Diane. Will you beg me prettily not to take the cane myself and give you another ten?"

"Yes! Please no more!" It was a desperate hasty mumble.

"My name, you wretch! What's my name?!"

"Madam! Please, Madam! No more! Don't beat me any more!" The words poured from her parched lips without thought.

"Very well. I'll have you fucked instead."

Abruptly her head was released and she banged her face against the bench as the muscles in her neck were taken by surprise.

She felt a hand groping roughly between her labia, even amidst the fires that still raged over her buttocks.

The fingers opened her with some difficulty and then felt inside her.

"She's dry, Madam," came a male voice.

"She'll learn. Stir her up and then fuck her. Sven, you next! Max, after him! Bernt you finish her off. If she's got any fire left after that, go round again. Then put the stuck up bitch back in her cell. I'm going to break her completely!"

Diane heard the words in dumb shock but before she could do anything, she felt the fingers go deep into her and begin to twist and clench, to stroke and stimulate her inside, so that she was helpless to prevent her tissues from responding mindlessly and she moaned in despair as she heard herself begin to squelch. The men laughed and Diane knew her vagina was going to get every bit as much of a pounding as her bottom had.

The first man enjoyed her humiliation to the full, forcing her cunt to continue to make hungry sucking noises around his fingers. Below her she saw the men's shoes as they all came to stand close to her and enjoy her disgrace. And strangely, even as she felt outrage and agony balancing the undeniable stimulation in her genitals, Diane also found a strange mental excitement at picturing herself, bent naked and vulnerable, punished before these men who would now take their pleasure with her. It was as if the very nub of her humiliation was somehow the cause of a strange excitement. Behind her she felt the broad pressure of the first man's cock replace his fingers. She felt her lips part for him moistly and he was able to slide in quite smoothly.

She had never experienced anything like it before. All the aspects of sex that she had thought essential were stripped away; there was no human contact, no affection, no foreplay, no tenderness. Instead there was the beating pain in her flogged backside, soreness from her wrists and ankles from where she had been tied, a total inability to close herself to this anonymous invader and yet the pleasure caused by his arrogant intrusion was exquisite. He slid further and further into her in one slow but unstoppable lunge, halting only when he was right at the neck of her womb. Never before had Diane ever felt so completely conquered by a man's body. And yet never before had she felt so utterly a woman as she did when rough, male hands gripped her hips and the thick shaft inside her began to slide back and forth, seeking its own pleasure – careless of the woman it was penetrating.

The man moved faster and faster, slapping his pelvis against her sore backside and contributing to the contradictory feelings of pain, shame and blinding pleasure she was grappling with. And as his shaft rammed into her time after time, she began to realise she was beginning to climb towards orgasm, but before she could do much more than register the fact, the shaft stopped at maximum penetration and she felt the man twitch against her as he pumped himself into her depths, then he was gone so suddenly that it was all she could do not to howl with loss and shock. But almost as soon as she had jerked her head up, the next man was there. Briefly she felt his fingers fumble with her as he aimed himself at her opening and held her lips apart, then he was inside and thrusting immediately. She felt the first man's emissions ooze out past him and start trickling down her thighs, but that only spurred her on. She ought to have been horrified. She had never taken two men in quick succession, and only once, when she had been a student had she had two different men in a week, let alone within five minutes. But far from horror, she was gripped by a ferocious desire to experience the peak of the climax she could now feel growing inside her, feeding off the pain of the caning and the incessant thrusting in her cunt. It was something more violent and intense than she had ever felt before. She whimpered as the second man slammed into her to spend himself and then withdrew.

Desperately she threw her head up and craned it round to watch the third man take his place. This time her cunt made a farting noise as the cock barged into her through the oozing sperm and then he was plundering her but she was dismayed to find that the men's laughter and her own shame only fed the fires within her. Her vagina was so soaked in her own emissions and in the spunk of the two previous men that it slowed her pleasure down, but to balance it, the man's cock was practically floating inside her and wasn't making such close contact with her inner tissues. As a result he too was on a longer fuse and Diane was agonisingly close to what she knew was going to be a climax like no other she had experienced when he stopped pistoning and clasped her to him while he spent and then he too was gone.

She couldn't help whimpering audibly and wagging her bottom as much as she was able – urgent for another cock. The men saw it and she got a ringing smack on a haunch from the fourth man.

"Okay. You take me for a good ride," he growled in a German accent. Then she felt him slide into her as another spurt of semen was squeezed out. This one was the biggest of the cocks by far and Diane was quickly caught up in the ascent to ecstasy again as the huge thing speared her and ploughed her to her neck. He was urgent himself however and wasted no time in gripping her hips and thumping into her. She had never been fucked so roughly but she was past caring and rushed headlong into a vortex of delight that threatened as much as it promised.

Diane screamed as her orgasm broke, shattering her mind and shocking every fibre of her body with its intensity – it was almost too much to bear and she was still shaking and moaning as she felt the man inside her pull out and spurt himself up her back.

She lay still, her heart thundering in her chest and her breathing deafeningly loud. She could feel her vagina quivering and clenching in the wake of the onslaught, her backside still throbbed and stung, her nipples had been rubbed almost raw as she had been rocked backwards and forwards by the successive fucks. But it had been the most devastating moment of her life. Suddenly a hand gripped her hair again and her head was dragged up so that she was staring at a large blond man.

"You reckon she still got fire in her, Sven?" It was the German who had had her last. Another blond man looked over his shoulder.

"She's still awake. I'd say that's fiery, so maybe we'd better do what Madam said."

Blearily Diane recalled something about 'going round again', her eyes widened in alarm as she realised that being gangbanged for a second time was really on the cards.

"No, please! Please......" She couldn't frame the words; her lips were dry and her breath caught in her throat.

"Sure!" the German said, smirking nastily. "You ask us nice. We do it."

He stood up and to Diane's utter dismay unzipped his flies and took out his flaccid length of cock, still glistening with its own emission and hers. He stepped forwards and presented it to her lips.

"'Course, we could always cane you instead....." he left the threat hanging and Diane hastily licked her lips, curbed her disgust and opened her mouth. He slid in and immediately began to thicken and harden as he felt her softness caress him. Diane struggled to relax as the cock continued to grow and push towards her stretched throat. She gave a muffled squeal as she felt another cock touch her buttocks and then find her entrance before pushing in once more on the lubrication of her previous use. In her mouth she was fighting not to retch on the thick, sour taste of the coating on the German's cock.

Christ! In her mind she shrieked as she realised that for the first time in her life she was taking two men at once.

And as if that wasn't enough to contend with, the man fucking her treated her buttocks to three tremendous slaps which fanned the embers of the cane-seared fires and set them blazing again. But she didn't have time to register that discomfort much because the German started coming.

She felt his massive shaft swell and twitch and then she panicked as thick, slimy sperm splashed into her mouth and she desperately tried to swallow. Her position just made it impossible however, and she spluttered helplessly as the huge cock seemed to go on and on pumping the stuff into her. She was choking and crying when it was finally withdrawn and she was able to draw in great breaths of air just in time to receive another load up her back and then yet another man slid into her burning and stinging vagina.

When that man finished she came again as he spent inside her. She had hardly ended her cries of climactic release as another shattering overload hit her, when yet another flaccid cock slid into her mouth and eagerly she set about preparing it for action again. She lost all conscious thought as her ordeal went on and the men used her at both ends time and again.

They had to carry her back to her cell when she was finally released and her legs refused to carry her.

When she woke the following morning, her face, legs, back and groin were crusted thickly with dried sperm, her backside stung and her cunt burned. But strangely there was no feeling of outrage or shame; just an unsettling knowledge that she had orgasmed more fiercely and more often than ever before.

Later that day she was flogged for the first time.

CHAPTER 3

To Amelia's delight she was being taken to an auction. At the Saturday morning meeting, Carlo had told everyone that there was a sale in Scotland the following week and he intended to see if there was anything worthy of filling either or both of the two spare stalls in the CSL stable. In case there was, he intended taking Amelia to look after the purchases.

The burly Spaniard had frowned when he was told of Chrissie Sands' opinion regarding Blackie when Patti reported it.

"That means she'll be injured for the games week after next!" he said.

"Run Ayesha instead," Brian suggested.

"Could do, I guess. But that'll mean she'll take maybe three weeks to heal up if there are any close races and the driver has to use the whip hard. And I know she's going to be hired out again before that. "

"Legs is shaping up well enough as all rounder, field her for now and then let's hope there's something good up for sale!" Tony concluded and Carlo agreed.

There was a final report on Cherry's bad behaviour of the previous day, although she had been quite placid so far that morning. Carlo recommended that she be sent up to The Lodge that evening after dinner, for the members to play with in the Common Room.

"That should settle her down again. And anyway tomorrow's the last day for playing before the next event, so she'll have a decent weekend's use to keep her going," he told the staff, standing up and stretching to signal the end of the meeting.

The trainers set off for their customary round of golf while the grooms set about tacking up for the usual pony work. Carlo always allowed his slaves one day a week off hard training. On Saturdays, rain or shine, the grooms took them for light pony work and for the remainder of the day they could rest in their stalls or if Patti felt in a good mood some of them were allowed to play with other slaves in their stalls.

It was a cold and crisp day and once the harnesses with their greased butt plugs were buckled on tightly and the bridles were settled with their bits going tidily through the slaves' tongue rings, the poncho blankets were again used until the slave was properly warmed up.

Amelia's first drive was the big German girl, Trouble. She was not a natural pony but a trot in harness was a good workout for a girl whose life was mainly spent in the training arena keeping her whip skills honed. She was quiet enough once she was between the shafts, especially as Helga was driving Ox alongside her. The two were inseparable and Trouble only really lived up to her name when she hadn't been allowed to play with her lover or hadn't been in an arena recently.

The two big blondes pulled the traps strongly and at a stately pace past the training centre and then their drivers took a right turn which led them down onto the road that led to the lake behind the big house.

Amelia felt work-related, city stresses drain out of her as the leather seat warmed under her thighs and a cool breeze fanned her face. The parkland looked stunning in its autumn plumage and the water of the lake was so dark and still it perfectly mirrored the fair weather clouds that floated above it and every leaf of every tree that stood on its banks. The leather of the reins jerked slightly in her hands as Trouble occasionally turned her head just a little. The wheels of the trap rumbled on the tarmac and hid the padding of the slave's bare feet. Beside her, Helga likewise ran

Ox on a loose rein, the whip just hovering over her shoulder.

Driving a pony was a joy that never paled for Amelia, she loved the tight lacing of the harness, the crupper strap bisecting and plumping out the labia, the tit straps keeping the breasts steady and, from behind, the bewitching sight of their buttocks rippling and swaying with every step. She shifted in her seat, uncomfortably aware that she was moistening and her arousal revived the stinging that Brian's attentions had left her with. She had been woken twice in the night to service him and before breakfast she had heaved a secret sigh of relief when he had decided to ejaculate into her mouth.

For no reason other than that she enjoyed doing it, she flicked the whipcord of the driving whip at Trouble's buttocks. Obediently the slave increased speed slightly and Amelia hauled back on the reins to keep pace with Helga and Ox. She laughed for sheer pleasure and flicked again at the big blonde slave and then reined her in. She adored the way that slaves were there to be played with in any way anyone wanted and sometimes recently she had caught herself feeling slightly cheated that as Brian's personal slave, she would never be treated with such utterly casual ease and cruelty.

Trouble shook her head and stamped for a few paces to show her annoyance at being given contradictory instructions so Amelia whipped her a few times across her bottom to quieten her.

Helga gestured towards a large oak that stood by the lake and they drew the two traps off the road and under its shelter. The two blonde ponies were now well warmed and their breath hung in clouds about them as the grooms unbelted the ponchos and took them off, stowing them in the small boxes behind the traps' seats. Amelia played with Trouble's erect nipples for a while, nipping at the rubbery tubes with her sharp teeth then pulling and twisting them. In between her blinkers the German slave's eyes closed briefly in pleasure and Amelia wished she could clamp the nipples. Being in pain always made a pony more spirited, in her experience.

But Saturdays were for gentle exercise and the slave was thoroughly welted from her whip training and so, reluctantly, Amelia climbed back onto her seat and took up the reins.

"Do you ever envy them, Helga?" she asked.

"What, the slaves? No, except when they're getting all the Masters' attention," the other girl replied with a broad grin.

"But that's what's so wonderful. Even when they're being played with, they don't really exist for the Masters. They're just.....things!...for giving pleasure. Totally anonymous, just existing to have things done to them....." Amelia's voice trailed off and Helga laughed.

"I think I'd get bored!" she said.

She whipped up Ox and steered back onto the road. Amelia sat for a moment, surprised at her own words. She hadn't fully realised that she felt like that. But Trouble stamped and fretted, eager to be off after Ox and Amelia smiled fondly and whipped her up.

A mile or so further on they met Anna Marie and Raika driving Ayesha and Blondie, coming the other way around the park. The four of them stopped and talked for a few minutes as the slaves' bodies and breath steamed. Feet raked at the tarmac impatiently, heads nodded and shook as the famous slaves fretted at being immobile on what should be their run. Amelia knew that at that moment they were the envy of any number of girls around the world who would have given everything to be where they were; driving four of the most famous arena slaves, casually hushing the great Blondie herself with a flick of a whip or curbing Ayesha – almost as famous – by a jerk of the reins; laughingly pulling Ox and Trouble apart when they tried to nuzzle too affectionately.

Then they parted company and trotted on, Amelia and Helga following the road that ran in front of the house and across the golf course. On the ninth green, Carlo, Brian and Tony were just holing out and heading for the tenth when the traps came by. There was another short pause as the men patted and teased the slaves, stroking the breasts and pressing the crupper straps to the clitorises. There was no harm in teasing the ponies and making the trot home a little more lively.

And as it turned out Amelia had to practically lean back on the reins from there on, and wrap flicks of the whip at Trouble's breasts to pull her back as she eagerly followed Ox back to the stable.

By the time the slaves were given their mid day feed, all of them had been run, and the staff spent the afternoon cleaning tack and taking various slaves into other stalls. They all had their favourites and would happily help things along by the introduction of strap-ons and dildos.

Amelia amused herself for an hour or so with Tigre and Purdy; having the big titted brunette kneel in her straw with her head down while she helped the gypsy girl kneel behind her with a strap-on buckled to her waist. She fingered Purdy's cunt into a welcoming lather before feeding the strap-on into it.

She stood behind the gypsy and played with her tits while she fucked Purdy, then she swapped them around and played with Purdy's large and heavy tits while she fucked Tigre. From all around her came the sounds of female orgasm as the slaves all climaxed repeatedly. In the end Amelia joined her moans to those of the others as Purdy knelt in front of her and gave her clitoris the tongue lashing it had been needing all afternoon.

Anna Marie was left on duty and Amelia and the others were allowed to dress in their Housegirl uniforms and attend the men at dinner that night. The dining room was a sight that should have delighted Amelia as her Master, resplendent in his dinner jacket, led her in on his arm, behind Carlo and Patti who in turn came behind John Carpenter and his wife. Champagne corks popped and the light from the chandeliers shone on naked female shoulders and the upper slopes of breasts, as Housegirls who were on waitress duty bustled about, and those who were there to escort the men smiled and made conversation.

Brian was in his element as various men from neighbouring tables asked about how this or that slave was faring in the warm up for the next events in the arenas. His and Tony's advice was sought on all aspects of the arenas and how bets should be placed, and from the opposite side of the table, Eve, who was Tony's slave, gave her a 'isn't this marvellous?' smile and she tried to return it. She loved the dress, of course she did and she knew that after the meal, either her Master or any of the members would enjoy playing with the breasts so temptingly offered up by the tight bodice. The cunningly hidden slit at the back of the skirt would enable any man to play with her cunt. And all around her was wealth, elegance and laughter, given added piquancy by the knowledge that later on, delicious debauchery would reign.

But all she could think of was the slaves settled in their stalls, not even knowing that the following day they would be offered for dungeon play at knockdown prices. It was the last day's play before training began in earnest. She felt a warmth in her belly at the thought that it was none of their business what was done to them and had to make an effort to drag her attention back to her Master when she felt his hand on her knee.

She travelled in the back of the horsebox on the long run up to Scotland, which was no hardship. There were two comfortable seats and a toilet as well as the stalls. They left before full light on the Tuesday morning and Amelia slept for the first three hours or so. The weekend had turned out to be an exhausting one. Saturday night in the Common Room had been so debauched that Amelia's sombre mood had been submerged beneath a tide of brilliant orgasms as many of the members had welcomed her back. She had been stripped and hung by her wrists from one of the rope and pulley systems that had been put in in place of some of the original chandeliers. Her arms had hurt savagely despite the suspension cuffs, and being stung into swinging and twisting as the whip cut at her only made matters worse. When she was taken down, it had only taken the briefest of fingerings to make her come, much to the amusement of the men, most of whom had turned their attentions to administering an exquisite breast beating to the black haired beauty who had been on reception just the previous evening. Two of the men however had remained to play with her and spread her out on one of the chaises longues then taken turns to have her. She had returned to her Master and Carlo dishevelled and adjusting her dress, breathless from her third orgasm.

For a while she had been able to sit with them and watch as the dinner jacketed men stripped and played with Housegirl after Housegirl, the huge room being superbly decorated with their hanging forms, slender and graceful, gleaming palely as they twisted under the lashes. Their cries of orgasm filled the room, spiralling upwards with the rich cigar smoke. Several men borrowed her to give oral service and her heart soared as she glimpsed the pride her Master took in watching her kneel before other men and open her soft lips wide for them. She knew she was in for a delicious beating when they got home. He didn't disappoint her, she was made to bend over naked and rest her hands on the seat of the sofa in his lounge. He watched a film on television and whenever he felt bored, he caned her. It was exactly the sort of usage Amelia was increasingly responding to. His casual fingerings in between canings left her juicing all the more because of their carelessness. The strokes he laid on her hurt appallingly as he took great pleasure in crossing over the welts from earlier and she appreciated being allowed to cry out under them and give her Master pleasure.

Sunday had been difficult for her; it was a tradition that before the slaves went into hard training before an event, they were allowed to give service in the club dungeons and the normal fees were heavily discounted to ensure that all of them were thoroughly used.

For the grooms it meant that they were almost worked off their feet, lacing various slaves into corsets, setting them on their best, five inch heeled, court shoes, slipping stockings up their legs and even applying make up. Then, on a leash that ran forwards from their clipped-together wrists and between their stockinged thighs, they were led up to the house.

Amelia got to lead none other than Blondie, the most successful and famous of all arena slaves. She was positively salivating at the thought of what the ingenious masters would get up to with her and was hoping she might be able to stay and watch. But as she led the tall blonde along the basement corridor which ended in the door to Dungeon Seven, the slave's high heels clicking on the stone and her sensational hips swinging, her breasts mounded up by the half cups of the basque, Amelia saw that Ivan, one of the mute Russian twins who were The Lodge's main security was waiting at the door. He took the blonde's leash from her and gestured her away. Four more times she led slaves up to the dungeons but never once was she allowed in.

All the grooms could do was to sit about and wait for the exhausted slaves to be brought back. To make matters worse, Patti was in a bad mood because Carlo hadn't taken her to one of the sessions either and so she forbade any play between any of them.

Amelia had envied the slaves as she had soaped them and showered them later on, spreadeagled and chained under the frames that ran on rails across the stable block's ceiling. They all carried livid welts and flares where the Masters had dealt out punishment. Some carried little marks where needles had been inserted and all wore the same, soft, look of slaves who had been well beaten and fucked. The most she could do was, in the guise of making sure each body had been thoroughly cleaned, insert her fingers deep into each vagina and enjoy its thick, soupy contents before she douched it. However, Patti had noticed and reported her to Brian for malingering.

Knowing a good thrashing was exactly what she was after, he had taken her to his bed for the night and then sentenced her to spend the whole of Monday chained to the whipping post in the centre of the yard. It had rained heavily and she was naked.

Only when it was nearly dark and she was shivering and miserable did he relent and take the whip to her. It was the most exquisitely painful beating she had ever undergone and satisfied even the most extreme of the longings that had been plaguing her.

As she thought about it in the horsebox, she pressed her thighs together as she recalled the wet lash clubbing across her back and buttocks until she had had no choice but to try and twist around. Then her thighs, stomach and breasts had taken their share. Showered and dried, she had taken her Master in all three holes, grateful and respectful for his hard work in disciplining her and the skill with which it had been done.

They arrived at the estate in mid-evening. An imposing stone house with mullioned windows under a slate roof, it stood in a valley above which moorland soared in all directions.

The CSL horsebox took its place among other big camper vans and horseboxes and as Amelia stepped out into the chilly evening, feeling her welts sting as she moved after her long confinement, she also felt a tingle in her groin as she surveyed the stables and knew that they contained maybe a hundred beautiful and submissive slaves, docilely awaiting their owners' pleasure.

After a buffet supper and a drinks party in a drawing room almost on a scale to rival The Lodge, they went to bed and Brian made her day by lending her to Carlo for the first part of the night. The casual way in which he had spun her around and pointed her towards Carlo's room, then smacked her bottom to make her trot off on her mission, was just so humiliating she wanted to fall to her knees and kiss his feet in gratitude.

Carlo repaid Brian's generosity with an energetic rogering followed by buggery, his fingers gleefully digging into her welts as he ploughed her to two massive orgasms before he spent in her backside and sent her back. She knew better than to shower before she had displayed herself to her master, to ensure he was satisfied that good use had been made of her. He merely grunted his approval and turned over in bed. He was fast asleep by the time she returned from the shower and Amelia felt her heart would burst with gratitude – if only he could always remember to be so cruel!

The viewing was held straight after breakfast which was taken in a dining room that had spectacular views over a tumbling river that ran across the estate. The owner, a bluff and friendly Scotsman whom Amelia recognised from The Lodge, came over to their table and chatted for a while, it transpired that Carlo had brought some of the CSL slaves here for extra training in the recent past. They had been released from the stableyard and then hunted down by men on horseback. He thought it had been the making of Blackie and Rose particularly.

The various companies that had grown up alongside the arenas and which specialised in auctioning their slaves, prided themselves on the ingenuity with which the merchandise was displayed and the ease with which prospective buyers could inspect it.

At this particular auction which was held in an echoing, stone built coach house, the slaves were exhibited on dildo poles. Their legs had been spread and their ankles chained down to either end of a crossbar, the pole had then been pumped up until their legs were stretched to optimum amounts for the inspection of musculature. Their arms were stretched out to the sides and their wrists shackled to cuffs that in turn were connected to a light yoke that ran, via a ring on the back of their collars, across their shoulders. A large ball gag ensured silence and the threat implied by electrodes clipped to their labia ensured that each slave remained still and upright. Any slouching was rewarded by a shock delivered straight to the cunt, and Amelia noted that most of the slaves' eyes were wide and worried. She would have bet that the guards had been giving the goods several demonstrations of what would happen if any of them slumped by so much as a millimetre.

Carlo and Brian went into professional mode as soon as they entered the building. Each slave's pole was mounted on a swivel so that they could be spun and examined minutely from all angles. From between each pair of buttocks a narrow rubber hose ending in a bulb protruded and Amelia instantly realised that an inflatable butt plug had been provided to assess the slaves' rectal capacities.

Almost by accident the arenas had realised that as they built up their squads of slaves, in between events in the arenas themselves, the slaves could earn their keep in other ways. Now an arena slave was not only a trained athlete, she also had to be a three hole submissive whore.

Carrying a notepad so that she could record any preferences or comments the men wanted, Amelia trailed around as Carlo felt biceps and talked about triceps and pecs. Her Master seemed more concerned with seeing how far the butt plugs could be inflated and checking on the length and smoothness of thigh.

All round her, men were earnestly discussing the commercial and pleasure potential of naked females who had no say in the uses to which they would be put. She felt a familiar tingle of arousal in her belly at that thought. It was made all the more exciting for her by the knowledge that each woman carried a chip at the nape of her neck that detailed her talents, achievements, discipline record and previous owners. To Amelia that was almost unbearably erotic, the thought that men had created a system so complete that their dominance stretched to the extent of rendering women into livestock and commodities. She had always found the arenas thrilling but now she was increasingly becoming certain that what she longed for was to throw herself utterly into the arms of that system and abandon herself completely to it. It was as if she was some kind of addict and that cruelty was her drug of choice. Nowadays she was irritated by anything other than full on humiliation and the most casual, brutal treatment.

Her master interrupted her thoughts as he straightened up from examining a brunette's crotch.

"Make a note of this one's number, Amelia," he told her. Obediently she went round to the slave's front and looked at the laminated card pinned to her left breast, it gave a printout of the information that could be confirmed by checking her chip and it also noted her number as being twenty-nine. Large, docile, hazel eyes regarded her as Carlo and Brian moved on.

"Lucky!" she whispered, and followed the men.

By lunchtime they had decided there were four slaves that might complement the CSL line-up. Presently, Ox, Trouble and Fiji would strengthen any stable that hired them in for the endurance events under the whips, like log pulling and whip duelling. Blondie and Ayesha were bankers for everything from chariot racing to dressage and could be relied on to out perform virtually any other slave on the circuit when it came to the prestige events like duelling with studded whips and 'Last Slave Standing'. Tigre, Cherry, Blackie, Rose and Beast were stalwarts for bolstering squad events without necessarily being star solo fighters. Legs, Jet and Purdy were best used as part racers and part solo fighters in the pens. For the two who would complete the CSL squad for the moment at least – although John Carpenter was already talking about expanding - Carlo was looking for girls who could serve in squad events like the mass log pulls and assault course running and also perform well in solo contests. That way he felt he could offer the big stables an across-the-range service to bolster all aspects of their performance.

Amelia knew from overheard conversations that both men were also acutely aware that Blondie and Ayesha could not go on for ever and they were constantly searching for that elusive star quality that one day they would need.

The auction proper was held in the yard. The auctioneer stood on a podium beside the stable door and introduced each lot which was then led out and paraded around a makeshift ring of wickerwork hurdles while prospective buyers leaned on them and placed their bids. Each slave was led out on a leash that ran forwards from her pinioned wrists and between her legs, they were quite naked apart from high-heeled sandals, collars and restraints. Their handlers, big men dressed in rough tweeds, had them walk and trot around the circle while the trainers and owners discussed the gait and the build of each one.

Lot twenty-nine impressed everyone with her long, relaxed stride and proud carriage.

"She's a beaut, Carlo!" she heard her master whisper to his boss.

Carlo made no reply except to nod slightly as he watched the bidding begin and the girl was led round and round, her handler squeezing her breasts and slapping her rump to illustrate the quality and fitness of the merchandise. Amelia watched Brian get more and more agitated as Carlo failed to enter the bidding and the amounts being offered became jaw-droppingly huge.

Eventually Carlo made a complicated gesture to the auctioneer which was obviously a pre-arranged signal because the minute the auctioneer saw it, he advanced the bidding by several thousand pounds in one fell swoop.

That cleared out all but two other bidders who valiantly tried to stay with Carlo but CSL had acquired formidable cash reserves and twenty-nine – or 'Lucky' as Amelia thought of her, was bought.

From then on Carlo became more cautious with money. They bid for a blonde who was lot thirty-seven but lost her to the trainer of a stable in the Far East. Lot sixty-three also escaped them but lot eighty-one they got. She was a redhead, heavily freckled right down to her cleavage; she was slender but Carlo was certain she had a wiry strength to her. And in any case she had a fiery look about her that suggested she hadn't been fully subdued just yet. In fact her discipline record was not good but that didn't put Carlo off. CSL had to a large extent made its reputation by being small enough to take on misfits and rejects and forge them into brave and tough competitors in the arenas and passionate submissives in the dungeon. Purdy, Trouble and Beast had been almost uncontrollable when they had been bought but had been transformed and tamed by CSL's ability to give them time and attention.

By the time all the lots had been disposed of and Brian and Carlo had rather smugly visited their purchases in their stalls, it was too late to start the journey home and so it was early the next morning, straight after breakfast when Amelia was dispatched to load the horsebox.

The slaves had been fed, watered and sluiced down and Amelia just ran a brush through Lucky's hair and attached her leash – spending a few moments investigating her vagina which turned out to be surprisingly capacious and moist to her questing fingers.

"If that's your usual state, my girl, I bet the Masters just love you after a beating!" she chuckled as she led her charge quietly out and into the box, where she settled her down on the straw and clipped her wrists to the partition between the stalls.

Brian had christened the redhead 'Sam' after a redheaded cartoon character and as soon as she entered her stall, Amelia knew she was going to be difficult. Baleful green eyes glared at her from under the thick, tumbling mane of flame red hair.

Amelia put her hands on her hips and cocked her head; thoughtful for a second.

"Okay then. You reckon 'cos I'm a girl that I'll be easy to mess around, yes?"

The slave just continued to glare and stamped a foot. Amelia shrugged and walked closer.

"I can whip just as hard as a man," she said, mentally making a note to confess this lie to her Master later on. "And where you're going, they've broken tougher ones than you'll ever be. Trust me on this!"

There was the slightest flicker of uncertainty in the girl's eyes and Amelia pounced, darting behind the slave and grabbing a handful of hair then jerking backwards savagely. The girl cried out and staggered backwards, her pinioned hands behind her making her willing to drop to her knees rather than risk falling. Amelia stood over her, legs spread and triumphant. One of the staff grooms looked in.

"It's okay thanks," Amelia panted. "She's just frisky."

As if to belie that verdict the slave tried to jerk her head free but Amelia exerted her strength and held firm, straining the slave's head back until the green eyes, watering with pain were staring up at her. She smiled down grimly.

"You just earned yourself a good beating, my beauty!" she panted, and without letting go of the hair she used one hand to clip the lead onto one of the wrist cuffs and kicked it forwards between the slave's legs. Then with no warning she rammed the slave's head forwards. Taken completely by surprise, the redhead ended up face down in her bedding while in one swift movement, Amelia leant down and picked up the handle of the leash, then she stepped from behind the slave and jerked the leash forwards and upwards. The leather bit deeply into the girl's crotch and with another cry she reared back and stumbled up onto her feet, panting and dishevelled.

Smiling proudly, Amelia led her sullen charge out of the stable, up the ramp and into the horsebox. She steered her carefully into her stall, pulled the leash back from between the shapely thighs and taking a short grip on it, she jerked it upwards, forcing the slave's arms up behind her and making her bend forwards. The redhead obviously knew what was coming and strained as hard as she could to resist the pressure. Amelia gritted her teeth and heaved again. For a moment it was an impasse and then Amelia felt the gym-trimmed muscles in her arm take the pressure and return it. With a strained grunt of effort she applied her full strength and forced the slave's arms up until with a wail of despair she collapsed forwards, her head buried in the straw and her hindquarters raised and offered for the whip. Amelia wound the leash around a hook on the stall's back wall to keep her immobile and stood back. The girl was good material. She knew she was beaten and had parted her thighs – obviously in response to training that emphasised the probable conjoining of fucking with beating – she had a good strong back and the sinews in her arms stood out as the leash strained them up behind her kneeling form.

Amelia smiled as she took down a crop, she had heard the remarks the men had made about how strong they suspected this one was, but her own workouts had stood her in good stead and she had beaten a promising arena slave in a straight contest of strength.

She delivered six heavy lashes with the crop while deep in thought and didn't pay that much attention to the cries and wriggling going on beneath her as she laid them on. Should she talk to her master about all the thoughts that were assailing her just recently? The trouble was he just wasn't in a position to help her achieve what she was rapidly coming to believe was her ultimate ambition. It was beginning to look as though she was going to have to take matters into her own hands once more. After all it had been her own decision to investigate the arenas in the first place and that was how she had met Brian. It saddened her that she would now almost certainly have to leave him behind, but in time he would understand.

She was just hanging the crop back up and admiring how the girl's vagina had blossomed and opened under the beating when Carlo and Brian appeared.

"Just had to keep this one honest," she replied when they asked if she had had any problems, then she buckled her safety belt on in her chair and pulled out a magazine to read as the ramp was folded up and they pulled away.

The two men took it in turns with the driving and when they changed over, the one coming off duty would come back and mouthfuck one or other of the slaves. On the way up, Amelia had enjoyed providing that service but now all she could do was watch enviously as the new stock was put through its paces.

Sam was released from her strained position and seemed to have learned her lesson, kneeling up obediently as Brian approached her with his cock already out.

"Maybe we could let this one grow a bit of pubic fuzz, just on the mound," he called back to Amelia as he held the redhead's face to his groin and bucked his hips carelessly. "If it's as good a shade of red as her head hair, it might catch the judges' eyes in dressage." He broke off suddenly as his face softened and he clasped the redhead even closer. Amelia watched carefully as the slave's throat worked with no more than the occasional strained sound of suction at her lips as the cock bucked while it discharged.

She well knew her master's proportions and was impressed by the technique and practice that must have gone into such a smooth performance. As soon as he had finished, her master pushed the slave away and zipped himself up, then went back to the cab, just squeezing one of her breasts as he passed.

Amelia looked at the redhead who was licking her lips and smiling; nameless, naked, kneeling and restrained, a chip in her neck carrying her past with her, destined for branding, tongue ringing and suffering for onlookers' and owners' pleasure for as long as she was sexually useful with only a number to identify her......

"I reckon you're both lucky," Amelia whispered.

The newcomers were duly branded and their tongues pierced and ringed the following afternoon before the usual crowd from The Lodge that the procedures attracted. The brands – a rectangle with the letters CSL inside it – were applied high up on one hip and after that trauma the tongue ringing was accomplished quietly and with a minimum of struggling or fuss.

And then, only forty-eight hours later, Amelia found herself driving back to London. At least she had got to see the inside of one of The Lodge's famous dungeons and to spend a couple of wonderfully painful hours there but this visit had been different, she knew that now. She had finally confronted and acknowledged the truth within her. This time she was leaving The Lodge firmly in her past and heading into a very uncertain future –but for the first time she felt happy returning to London – for now London was where she needed to be. And the uncertain future was what she wanted.

CHAPTER 4

Respectfully and carefully, Diane pressed her breasts together around the hard, ribbed shaft of the guard's cock. She thought it was Sven, she had been trained not to look up at whoever was using her, but really it didn't matter – all that mattered was that she was servicing someone in authority; and the people who ruled her life now could make her do whatever they wanted her to do.

She had learned that during the weeks – months? She had no idea of how long she had been kept in that dreary warehouse. The men – and Madam of course – dispensed pleasure and pain and rammed home to the inmates every day that it was entirely up to them which one they chose to bestow or inflict. It was up to the inmates to find what pleasure they could in any circumstances that confronted them.

It had come as an unpleasant shock, but an undeniable truth, to Diane that her body seemed to react eagerly to pain as a precursor to pleasure. And at least there were mind blasting orgasms when Madam allowed that to happen. Unfortunately when it didn't, the men took immense pleasure in watching her weep tears of frustration from within her cell as other women were taken out and used.

Madam said she was a star performer and often locked her back in her cell after one of the men had tied her to a frame and used a single tail whip on her back and buttocks until she was near an orgasm from the pain alone. Then when she was practically gushing over the fingers that assessed the state of her cunt, she was dragged, crying, back to her cell and left with her hands free while another woman took her place, was beaten and then fucked.

She masturbated frantically as she watched, her face pressed against the bars of her cell door. And Madam would stand just outside, grinning as she told her how many lashes she was earning. But Diane couldn't help herself.

It was as if she had suddenly realised why she had been born. Her body had been created to please by suffering and to experience rending pleasure as it did so, her mind had been quick to understand and appreciate the cleverness of the cruelties visited on her and to contrive to seek out every opportunity to experience that pleasure. Nothing else mattered.

Sex before her enslavement had been a poor thing, she now realised and was desperate to make up for lost time.

Now she knew how blindingly a woman could respond to pain, domination and sexual use, she wanted to experience nothing else.

So after the masturbation she would be led out and flogged, sometimes suspended by her ankles with her legs spread wide apart; sometimes on her breasts but if she wasn't fucked afterwards she would masturbate helplessly all over again. Madam's respect for her monetary value always kicked in long before Diane's determination to get full sexual satisfaction was achieved and she would often have to be chained immobile and gagged in her cell.

Apart from punishment and discipline sessions, all the inmates had jobs around the place. Some helped in the kitchens, some swept out the big room where the majority of the punishments took place and where her first caning had been inflicted.

Madam, having taken an initial dislike to Diane, had assigned her to cleaning out the men's toilets and there she had become acquainted with the full meaning of humiliation.

Alone of all of the women, Diane worked naked. That way she could be hosed down at the end of the day, which was the quickest way to clean her up. But she didn't mind. She loved the way the men would release the hot, hard, golden torrents over her face and tits. It was much better than the spray from a woman – and they had made her experience that as well. Anything was fine by her – just as long as the men enjoyed it and were more likely to take their pleasure with her. She knew the other captives despised her – even those who had been slaves previously - and that they only faked enough submission to have as easy a ride as they could. But in her turn she despised them and regarded them as foolish to deprive themselves of the spectacular landscapes of intense pleasure that complete submission could open up for them – as it had for her.

And then just this morning a new woman had appeared with Madam. Diane had been on her hands and knees scrubbing the concrete floor when she had heard two sets of high-heeled shoes tapping across the floor towards her, together with the heavier tread of a man.

"This is the one," she heard Madam say.

Diane kept on with her work, another part of her training had been to learn that conversations held about her had nothing to do with her directly. A finely crafted pair of dark blue, hand stitched high-heeled court shoes; shoes to die for, came into her view as she laboured on, looking down at the floor.

"It's got a reasonable figure. How well trained is it?" she heard the voice from above her say, it was every bit as refined as the footwear would suggest.

"It'll have done to it whatever I want," Madam said and a pair of men's shoes came into view as the female ones backed off.

"Shower her, then tit fuck her and have her suck you," Madam said and Diane felt a toe of one of her shoes prod her in a buttock. She was obviously being shown off for some reason or other but that didn't matter. What really mattered was that she was going to get played with.

She held still as she watched the trousers in front of her move as the man freed his cock and then there was the familiar and comforting hammer of liquid on her back and the golden drops splashed past her face as they sprayed off her. The man moved slightly and she felt the rain beat down on the back of her head and drench her hair into rat tails that quickly trailed down on either side of her face. She enjoyed that especially, it was so completely submissive to kneel with her head down and her hair matted and soaked.

The man finished and moved away. Diane braced herself for the hosing down and held steady against the icy blast of water as it sluiced her clean.

"Kneel up," Madam said and eagerly she obeyed, pushing her breasts together and using them to caress the rapidly hardening shaft of the man's penis – it was definitely Sven she realised, he had a mole about half way down one side of his shaft. She looked down proudly at her large soft mounds which she was using her hands to mould around him and tease him with, making them fold gently right over his glistening purple helm and then letting them roll down the length of his shaft. It was a technique that had cost her some exquisitely painful whippings to master. In fact Madam had first tumbled to how masochistic she was when she had realised that Diane was deliberately making the men come too soon expressly so that she could be punished. A horribly long time in solitary confinement with her hands restrained at all times to prevent masturbation had put paid to that manoeuvre.

"Suck!" came the terse command and with nothing but heartfelt enthusiasm, Diane let her breasts go and holding Sven's hips to steady herself she stuck her tongue out as far as she could and began to lick and swirl her tongue around the helm that tasted acrid and salty and totally delicious. She rolled her tongue and tried to get it deep into the meatus. She ducked her head and lapped as far down the shaft as his trousers would allow and only then, when she had made a good show of letting him see how eagerly her tongue caressed him, did she open her mouth wide and slowly let her soft lips engulf him. She didn't rush to take him down but moved slowly to prolong his pleasure, trying to stop her tongue from lapping him and hastening his ejaculation. She felt him lodge against the back of her throat and concentrated on relaxing as she pushed on and her throat began to caress him instead. Above her she heard him sigh. She felt large hands placed at the sides of her head and the thick, mouthfilling shaft began to slowly withdraw and then advance again.

Inwardly Diane was crying out for him to come, she loved the feel of the erupting, pumping cock and she loved the taste of sperm and how thick and slimy it was. It all fed her slavish desire to abase herself before her captors, her mentors, the people who controlled her and who had shown her what she truly was.

Suddenly she felt the hands increase their grip and she allowed her head to be roughly jerked lower, providing the final caress to begin his climax. He made a strained grunt just as she felt his cock swell and jerk. And then her head was used mercilessly as he fucked her mouth.

He yanked her brutally onto him as the sperm jetted out and she concentrated on relaxing to accommodate him and the thick spend he was pumping down her. His hands gripped fiercely in her hair as he came but she was able to lift away just enough to get a taste of his come in her mouth before he finished.

Sven pushed her away as he stepped back and she knelt back on her heels and awaited further developments.

"Not bad," came the polished, refined voice. "I'll see her whipped of course and then try her out myself."

"Of course," Madam replied and clicked her fingers. Diane knew the signal and stood up, taking care to keep her eyes averted downwards. Again the polished, hand stitched shoes came into view and she noted the smooth, shapely, nylon clad legs and designer labelled handbag. A beautifully tailored skirt hugged the thighs from about three inches above the knees. For the briefest of moments Diane experienced a pang of loss. They had been the clothes of her dreams – and she had owned some shoes not too dissimilar – but now they were lost to her forever. She understood that what had happened to her was irrevocable and if she was ever to wear anything beautiful or expensive again, it would be by someone else's decree and for their pleasure; not hers.

Sven's hand gripped her arm and propelled her towards the echoing space where all the main punishments took place. She made no attempt to pull back and only felt the usual increase in her pulse at the thought of a beating and being made to serve.

She was put in the tall frame, stretched out to the corners so that her feet couldn't touch the floor and she could feel the tension in her every sinew. The strange woman came to stand in front of her and because Sven had mounted her off the floor, Diane was able to see the woman's face peering up at her.

Her dark hair was tied back severely and her face was finely boned with quite prominent cheek bones; it was a face one could admire as being good looking, Diane thought, but it was hard. The eyes glittered darkly and the mouth was a little too thin lipped. She held Diane's face in gloved fingers that gripped her chin so that she could lock gazes with her.

"Beat her until I tell you to stop," she said coldly when she was sure she had Diane's full attention. If the woman had been hoping for a whimper of protest or despair, Diane was glad to be able to disappoint her. It had been some time since any of the men had been let loose on her and a beating to orgasm would complement the fellation nicely......if the woman would allow Sven to take her that far.

To Diane's surprise the woman didn't stand back when the whip fell. It was one she was no stranger to – a thick, braided, single tail with the spiteful tassels at its end that stung and bit at the sides of ribs and breasts when wrapped round its target from behind. Being suspended, Diane was unable to move much, even as the hot trails of agony seared her and that seemed to suit the woman, she watched closely as her breasts shook and trembled in the wake of the lash and didn't seem to mind risking her fingers getting bitten by the whip as she ran them over the wicked little dents and lacerations the whip made, even while Sven continued to play it across her shoulders and back.

Smack!

Smack!

Smack!

In the relentless, steady rhythm that was Sven's style. The heat and scorch of the lashes – she thought the tally had mounted to something over thirty – began to meld and blur into thrilling pleasure as the woman's gloved fingers stroked her breasts and ribs and traced the welts she had caused to be inflicted. As the teasing fingers slid downwards towards her spread thighs and Sven calmly and pitilessly worked the lash on her, Diane put her head back and dared hope that her tormentors wouldn't stop before the scarlet clouds of submissive orgasm engulfed her.

She shuddered as she felt the fingers reach her cunt.

The whip continued to fall; across her buttocks now, her hips and delta taking the sting of the tails.

The fingers ran lightly across the throbbing nub of her clitoris, knowledgeable and cruel, not stopping to bring release.

Sven started to whip the backs of her thighs.

The fingers gently eased her lips apart and slid into her effortlessly.

Diane groaned and thrust her hips forward as best she could.

"Stop!" the woman called.

The derelict space echoed to Diane's cry of frustration. So many lashes taken, so much pain absorbed. She deserved release! Groggily she opened her eyes and looked down into the woman's face; smiling a cruel little smile.

"Very impressive, Doctor Williams. How many lashes was that?" she said.

"Forty three," Sven told her.

The woman held her ungloved fingers up to her nose and sniffed Diane's juice then licked them clean, a pink little tongue emerging like a cat's from between perfectly glossed lips.

"Take her down and then leave us," Madam told Sven.

He unfastened her ankle cuffs and then gripped her tightly around the waist and supported her while he released the cuffs at her wrists. She gritted her teeth and stifled a gasp as his arm revived the havoc his beating had woken in her back, and then she was back on the floor on hands and knees.

Madam clicked her fingers again and Diane began to crawl towards the padded bench over which she had first met the cane.

Now however the strange woman and Madam were leaning back against it and as Diane crawled towards them the strange woman began to furl and gather her skirt up her long thighs and bunch it around her hips. Her legs were clad in black, hold up stockings and she was naked of any underwear. A well trimmed, dark bush of hair showed at the join of her thighs, which she now spread.

Serving a woman had come as almost as big a shock as finding she enjoyed being abused. At first she had felt sick.

She thought that all the prisoners had probably been put through it, but one afternoon she had been taken a room she had never seen before. Madam had reclined on a leather ottoman with a guard watching carefully. Diane had been released and pushed roughly into the room.

Madam had been wearing a simple silk wrap and had undone the belt and let it fall apart to reveal a pair of large, pale skinned breasts capped with deep red nipples and tawny areolas. She shifted a little and allowed her legs to fall apart. She was shaven completely at her crotch.

"Lick me," was all she said.

Diane had shaken her head, appalled at the prospect.

"It tastes surprisingly nice, little fool. Better than men, isn't that right, Bernt?"

The man had shrugged and smiled.

"Get used to it or I'll keep you in solitary until your hair goes white." Suddenly she sat up and became serious. "And don't make the mistake of thinking I can't do whatever I want to with you!"

The solitary cell was underground and Diane had already made its acquaintance. She had been kept shackled tightly and in the dark until she had learned not to ask for punishment to fuel her own desires, but to accept that she must submit to the pleasure of others. She had no intention of going back into the pitch blackness.

Slowly she had knelt before Madam and reluctantly approached her opened crotch, the thick outer lips of her cunt were divided by wavy lines of pink inner lips and Diane had been struck by the aromatic scent of arousal. She had let her nose and then her tongue touch the soft sexflesh and with one final shudder of distaste had licked. To her surprise, if she blotted out the notion of one woman pleasuring another and just concentrated on the taste, it wasn't too bad.

In time, she had driven Madam to orgasm with her tongue lapping at places she had never dreamed she would ever lick on any man, let alone a woman. She had been rewarded by prolonged attentions from the whips and the cocks of the guards.

Now she was obviously required to put her lessons into practice and she moistened her lips as she knelt up and prepared to tongue this stranger. She smelled more pungent than Madam and a small lick confirmed that she would be harsher and more animal tasting. That appealed to Diane and she buried her nose in the soft pubic fur and foraged for the clitoris which responded by erecting almost immediately. Harsh tasting juices began to wash over her tongue and Diane took a longer lick which encompassed the beginning of the woman's cleft and then, with a duck of her head she found her opening before returning to the clitoris.

"Not bad!" the woman conceded. "Play with yourself while you work on me."

Diane could have blessed her. Sven's beating had left her cruelly denied and the fires of his lashes were still raging between her legs. Her hands dived there immediately and she frotted her clitoris urgently with one hand while penetrating herself harshly with the other. Her tongue ground and rubbed at the woman's clitoris with unabated glee while she did so.

"Now stop playing with yourself!" the command was snapped out precisely and authoritatively, despite Diane having been sure she was near climax. With an inner wail of frustration her training made her drop her hands to her sides even as she went on licking and swallowing the spicy outpourings from the stranger's cunt.

An elegantly shod foot was raised and placed against her chest, pushing her away. Diane knelt back on her heels, aghast at the steely self control the woman was capable of demonstrating.

"She's good. Have Sven put her up again and then leave me with her for half an hour. Then you'll have my answer."

Diane allowed herself to be mounted once more, this time by two suspension cuffs buckled to her wrists and clipped to a single chain attached to a ceiling winch. As Madam and Sven left them alone the strange woman held the remote control and used it to pull Diane up until she was only just able to stand on tip toe.

Nervously Diane watched as the woman browsed among the racks of whips and instruments for inflicting diabolically effective torment on the female body. She had experienced most of them and wouldn't have minded a repeat performance with any of the guards but this woman's icy control made her nervous. Without turning round the woman undressed down to her stockings and high heels, picked up a venomous single tail and turned to face Diane.

Her body was trim and toned and yet still obviously soft and feminine but at her breasts, as if to counter any suggestion of too much softness she wore spiked nipple cones.

Holding the whip across her groin, she sauntered over to Diane, whose arms and toes had begun to ache.

"Doctor Williams says you're the best of the bunch this time. At least for my purposes."

She stood at almost exactly the same height as Diane and as she came close, Diane felt the tines on the cones prick her areolas. She pressed a little closer, making Diane gasp, partly in anticipation of more pain to come, partly in answer to the slight increase in pressure on her nipples. The woman's tongue snaked out and ran around Diane's lips, tasting her arousal, tasting her own juices.

"While I whip you, tell me about yourself. Who you were, what you did….." The instruction was a whisper as the woman's cheek rubbed her own. Diane felt the leather of the whip run across her lower stomach and trigger a warm flood inside her. The woman seemed to understand and Diane felt her hand, ungloved now, trail slowly down her stretched body and slip easily inside her.

She chuckled softly and smiled into Diane's grimace of strained pleasure.

"You might get lucky and be allowed to come!" she said and disappeared behind her, making her cry out again as the hand was withdrawn from within her cunt.

The woman's way of using the whip was quite unlike anything Diane had encountered up to that point. She strolled about behind her, firing questions off and then firing in lashes at random intervals. The result was that the customary excitement of being caused pain and being used by a dominant for their pleasure was very slow in coming and the pain very prolonged. But eventually she seemed to decide that she knew enough about Diane and set about a steady beating which she kept up long enough to allow her to orgasm, frantically trying to cross her thighs and rub them together as she danced under the lash at the end of her chain.

As she hung, panting in the wake of her climax, the woman came and embraced her from in front, making Diane groan in pleasure at the pain of the spikes on her nipples.

"So," she whispered again as Diane, grateful for her orgasm, kissed and licked her fragrant cheek. "I know that you used to be a recruitment consultant but what are you now? Hmm?"

Diane didn't have breath for an answer because the embrace was tightening and steel dug into her nipples while fingernails dug into her buttocks.

"You're a talented and beautiful masochist. And that's a very – valuable....thing......to......be!"

At each word the woman pulled Diane's body hard against her and thrust her chest at her, scoring her with the nipple cones and sending shards of white hot pleasure through Diane's exhausted body.

"I'm going to buy you," she told her eventually, stepping away. "I'll have a look at the others and see if there's anything I can use, but the next time you're let out of your cell, you'll be my property." She reached out and made Diane catch her breath as she seized a nipple and pinched it cruelly between fingernails. "It won't be an easy berth, but I guarantee it'll be interesting!"

CHAPTER 5

A melia knew that she had a clear hour to work in. Everyone, except for herself and Danny, had left and the office was deserted. Security wouldn't look in until seven o'clock at the earliest. She knew because Brian had sometimes come up to town and she had played the secretary to his boss and been disciplined in her own office.

As she examined her reflection in the long Ladies' bathroom mirror, she had to acknowledge just a slight pang of remorse that tonight she would take her first definite step away from him.

But she just couldn't go on living with her present level of discontent and frustration.

On her return from The Lodge, it had taken her over a month of careful planning and the use of her inside knowledge of the slave-trading scene to reach this stage. And it had also meant using Danny Mearns' long-standing but never acknowledged lust for her. She had been aware of his lingering glances and how he tried to get just a little closer to her at all opportunities than was strictly necessary; and it wasn't really his fault, she didn't tell anyone at work about her sexual tastes or that she had a master. As far as anyone there knew, she was unattached and fair game. So she had never encouraged him but had never been rude to him either; and tonight she hoped that was going to pay dividends.

All it had taken was a note asking him to stay late as she wanted to talk to him in private. She had had to gamble that he wouldn't blab to all his mates in the pub they inhabited at lunch and after work, but he seemed a quiet sort and she didn't often see him in there, so she kept her fingers crossed.

Now she stood back, put her lipstick in her bag and gave herself the once over. She certainly didn't look like a slave! She had selected a neat, crisp, pale yellow shirt to wear beneath her black skirt suit. It was the one she didn't often wear because it had a long jacket and a short skirt so that with the jacket on and buttoned up, it looked as though she wasn't wearing a skirt at all. It had come in useful on occasions when she wanted the men she was meeting on business to let their dicks do their thinking. After long consideration she had not brought stockings to change into, the skirt would show their tops and that would have looked too tarty; instead she had shaved them the night before and gone bare legged all day. Tights were just not to be considered for this mission!

Simple black court shoes finished the ensemble and she thought it looked pretty 'office seduction' credible.

Wishing herself luck she walked back along the corridor and into Danny's office without knocking.

He looked up and smiled.

"Hi.......er.......what?....er.........I mean take a seat......"

He must have spent the whole day imagining various scenarios, she thought and almost felt sorry for him as he stuttered and stammered and tried not to look at how many buttons on her shirt she had left undone. She ignored his confusion and walked straight to his desk, went round it and then hoisted herself up to sit on it just to his left. The short skirt rode up and she crossed her legs, just to put the icing on the cake.

Danny sat back in his chair, Amelia's thighs right beside him. She rested one foot on the arm of the chair.

"Do you want me, Danny?" she asked and then held up her hand as he started to search for words. "Don't worry, this is no wind up. I need something from you and I'm willing to pay you in any currency you want."

She leaned forwards so that he got a full look down her cleavage. "And I do mean in any currency!"

"Yeah! Okay, I fancy you. What do you want from me?"

"I'll tell you in a couple of days. In the meantime to show good faith, I'm willing to make some payment in advance."

She kept her eyes on him and shrugged off her jacket, then relaxed sideways so that she was lying on his desk and curled her legs up onto the desktop too.

"What I want from you will take some work, Danny. So starting here and now, I'm ready to do anything you want. Anything, Danny."

She reached forwards and stroked his cheek, then reached further to cup the back of his head and draw him to her. He came easily and she lay back, feeling his lips press firmly to hers and his tongue begin to quest inside her mouth. She felt his hand gently brush her breast, recoil uncertainly, but as she held him more tightly, it returned and softly explored its contours through her shirt.

It seemed like ages since any man had treated her so gently and she had forgotten what it was like to be taken so uncertainly and with such trepidation. It was quite a pleasant change she realised, but knew it would soon pall and she would once again need to be dominated, so Danny needed to be hustled along a bit.

She broke the kiss and smiled up at him.

"It's all yours. Really. All I'll need is your help in arranging a little journey I want to go on." She shifted her hips on the desktop to get her bottom under her a bit more and then drew her legs up so her skirt fell down her thighs to her crotch. A pale pink and girlie thong – chosen after long deliberation - was all that shielded her sex.

Danny, flushed and still unsure of himself – or maybe he was unsure of her, licked his lips and then slid his hand down her thigh and then under the scrap of lace to finger her slit and grope his way to her clitoris and her opening. As he explored her he became quickly more adroit and confident in his movements and Amelia didn't have to pretend pleasure when she felt his fingers begin to rub her clit and then pause while he yanked her thong out of his way. She lifted her pelvis to help him slide it off her hips and then leave it halfway up her thighs as he returned to feeling inside her and stimulating her clitoris.

As his desire came to the fore he progressively became more confident and sure of himself and she continued to encourage him. She reached out as he stood beside the desk and took hold of his cock through his trousers. It was impressively long, she discovered, and she made sure she told him so. That seemed to spur him on and, keeping one hand deep inside her cunt he used the other to start an impassioned mauling of her breasts.

That was more like it!

Amelia groaned in genuine pleasure.

"Go on, Danny!" she whispered in a brief break from their kiss. "I like it rough!"

She realised later that she must have fulfilled all his secret fantasies because he responded better than she could have dared hope. His hand clawed hard into her tit, making her gasp at the sudden, hard lance of pain that shot down through her to where his fingers suddenly started to jab spitefully into her cunt. She cried out in genuinely surprised pleasure and gripped his cock harder. Suddenly she was sharing his urgency, it had been a month since she had had a decent fuck after all, she told herself afterwards.

Danny took his eager hands off her long enough to rip his jacket off and his shirt. Amelia sat up, aware that now it came to it, a desktop was not the most comfortable place to be fucked. When she and Brian had role played in her office, the sessions had usually ended with her bent over the desk being taken from behind, but she thought that the caning which had always taken place prior to that was a bit too advanced for Danny just yet.

She looked around and saw his executive chair. She swung her legs off the desk and jumped down, then shed her thong, her jacket and shirt before Danny was on her again. He was bare footed and stripped to the waist, her bra was ripped off in the first few seconds of an embrace that soon had his fingers sliding easily back into her and gripping and twisting quite expertly.

"Chair! Go in from behind!" she whispered, her voice hoarse with need.

He was quick on the uptake and whirled her around before pushing her forwards so she could clamber up and kneel on the seat, facing the back, sticking her bottom out for him. Glancing back over her shoulder she saw him wrench his trousers and pants down and then advance on her with his cock wagging eagerly, its gleaming, purple helm aiming for her flooding entrance.

She turned back and closed her eyes to concentrate on the feeling and sighed in delight as he rammed himself into her and she felt herself filled to the brim and spread wide by a man again.

He bucked his hips against her bottom in a strong, regular rhythm that had his shaft reaching deep inside her and driving her masterfully up towards an orgasm that broke mercifully, just a few seconds before she felt him half collapse over her back, reach for her breasts and clench his hands into fists in them in time to his spurts inside her.

Sweat-soaked and naked, apart from her skirt rucked up into nothing more than a frill round her hips, Amelia slithered down the leather of the chair to lay her chest on it, while kneeling on the floor. Behind her, Danny stood panting triumphantly and looking down on her well-fucked form.

Hazily she framed the thought; Stage One completed.

The following night they bunched Danny's jacket under her bottom and found that the desktop was not too bad after all. The night after that she knelt in front of his chair and sucked him, taking down every drop of his sperm with more eagerness than he had ever encountered before. While not as thick as Brian's cock, Danny's was longer and had an interesting curve to it. His sperm tasted less salty than some who had used her mouth in the past but was just as satisfactorily thick and slimy as Brian's had been.

His admiration for her skill at fellatio allowed her to begin to teach him about her sexual tastes.

This was the part she had been dreading. She knew that most straight women and men would react with horror to her masochism and she felt that perhaps she ought to leave her involvement with the arenas until a little later.

As it was, Danny was quiet and thoughtful when they finally dressed and left the office the night she told him. All the following day, Amelia could hardly concentrate on her work, all her plans hung on Danny not being repelled by her nature. Eventually, at the end of the day she listened to everyone walking past her office on their way out, some stuck their heads round her door to wish her goodnight, but of Danny there was no sign as there had not been all day. With her heart pounding, Amelia went to the Ladies', took off her blouse, removed her bra, then replaced the outer garment with two more buttons undone, took her knickers off, combed her hair and prepared herself to be told she was a sickening pervert. She could handle the rejection, but she would certainly have to leave her job and it would seriously delay her plans concerning her long term future.

She entered his office without knocking and saw him seated at his desk. He was frowning at her and her heart sank until she saw that in his hands he held a doubled over leather belt. He snapped it taut and stood up.

"You're a slut, Amelia! Strip and bend over, legs spread. I'm going to punish you."

She smiled and obeyed with all her heart and was impressed by his vigour. He seemed to have taken her at her word and he didn't start off gently, he treated her like the experienced submissive she was and laid the leather on hard. As a result, she took a ferocious beating that left her marked and happy for a fortnight. Danny got a willing fuck and an even more willing suck, with the promise of buggery as and when he required it. In short, she began to make him understand that she would happily agree to absolutely anything he had ever wanted to do to, and with, a woman.

When they started using his flat, they logged onto the arena sites and it turned out that, like an increasing number of people who publicly scorned the depravity of the arenas, in private he was quite an avid fan. She told him about her involvement with CSL and The Lodge – carefully avoiding any reference to Brian – and he was stunned by how close she was to such a famous stable. Equally carefully she also told him about her fellow grooms and so was ready to overcome the very last problem.

"But if I help you do this, I might not ever see you again….." he said one night, his voice betraying the depth of unhappiness that would cause him. She finished off swallowing the load of sperm he had just spurted down her throat, licked her lips and fingers and, naked, sauntered across his lounge, knowing her welted back and bottom would hold his attention and probably have him hard again in minutes. She checked the time and rang a number stored in her mobile.

"Helga? Yes, it's me. Listen, you know you and Anna Marie want somewhere good to stay when you come up to town for your days off? Well, I've just met a very sexy dom who's got an amazing pad in Islington. Shall I give you his number?"

She looked across at Danny who was sitting up, naked, priapic and smiling broadly. She went back to him when she had finished the call and knelt in front of him again, leaning forwards to take little, teasing licks at his cock which hardened still further at her touch.

"Okay, tell me what you want me to do," he said.

"In a minute. I need my mouth for something else just now, while you decide which hole you want to come in next."

He chose her backside, it was still a novelty for him, but despite her best attentions and her willingness to spread her cheeks apart for him, he found it hard to agree to what she wanted and only eventually gave in when she got Anna Marie and Helga to send him photos of themselves.

He spent the next few evenings out, holding meetings with someone whose details she gave him and she made sure she was extra attentive to his every need when he returned. Then it all went quiet for a week or so and she had no alternative but to fret in silence and hope for the best.

Then one evening, when she was tied down on Danny's bed and awaiting a thrashing with his newest whip, the phone rang and she heard him talking seriously.

"That was him," he told her, coming back into the bedroom. "He's gone for it. They've been tailing you, taken photos of you and everything. They're actually going to do it!"

Amelia felt her stomach lurch with combined fear and excitement; exactly the high she needed and had been missing so much. She had put Danny in touch with a known middle man in the slave trading underworld, one who she knew, from talking with Brian and Carlo, supplied the main arena auction houses. Danny had posed as a ruthless businessman who was down on his luck but who had a good looking woman to trade. She had made it clear that he was welcome to keep what they paid him for her.

With a sense of growing disbelief that occasionally spilled over into fits of giggling at inappropriate times, Amelia helped with the plans for her own abduction. It was to take place in the car park at her block of flats. Danny would tell his contact when she was working late and she would be waylaid as she walked from her car to the lift. There didn't seem to be any problem with penetrating security and Amelia made sure she would be very late so there wouldn't be anyone else around.

Danny however was still uneasy about the irreversible nature of the step she was taking.

"What if you can't stand it two or three years down the line?" he asked one night, pausing in the act of placing a clamp on her labia.

Amelia unwillingly dragged herself down from the dreamy heights that the earlier beating and fuck had propelled her into and back into which the added pain was now propelling her even more deeply.

"Mmm? If I hate it I'll be crap at it and they'll sell me, we've been through this. Aaah! Yes!"

Danny allowed the clamp to grip snugly.

"Okay, you'll have a chip, all the slaves do now, so your details will be on record. Make sure you leave me contact details of all the auction houses you know. That way I can keep an eye out for you coming up for sale online. I know they won't record your real name, but I can spot dates and measurements and there's not much of your body I don't know now. Deal?"

"Yes, yes, deal. Now.......Aaah! Yes!"

Another clamp closed on her lip. If only he had progressed to needles! Still she would leave that to Anna Marie and Helga, they would show him the way soon enough.

A further week passed, until after an agonisingly long day at work and with a fond farewell having been taken with Danny, and letters having been written to Brian and all at CSL, Amelia parked her car in the gloom of the underground park below her apartment, her mouth dry, her heart hammering. There was no going back now.

She took her clutch bag, dropped her keys in it as usual and walked towards the lift. Her heels sounded thunderous in the deserted car park. How would they do it? Belatedly she wondered if they would hurt her. Like any sub she had no fondness for pain that wasn't sexual in some way. She was still pondering that question when a black bag was thrust down over her head from behind her. Strong hands gripped her arms, her jacket was ripped from her shoulders and she felt a sharp pain in one upper arm. She wriggled furiously, panicking in the claustrophobic darkness and then knew nothing more until she woke up naked.

CHAPTER 6

Diane only woke as her cell door was pushed open and one of the guards brought her breakfast in on the usual tin plate. She had been chained to her bed the previous night, her wrists fed through the bars of the bedhead and then fastened together. Her ankles had been chained apart and all the guards had fucked her when she had been returned from her new mistress' beating.

The coarse fabric of the sheet beneath her had scratched at her flogged back very nicely as man after man had plunged into her and lain on top of her. One of the other prisoners had been brought in to lick her clean after each fuck and all in all it had been a very satisfactory conclusion to her stay, she felt. It was definitely time she moved on. Her new mistress seemed to be much cooler and more inventively cruel than Madam.

Not that she wasn't grateful to Madam, she smiled as she sat on the edge of her bed and chewed the black bread, remembering how naïve she had been when she had first been abducted. Her horror of the strip club was nothing short of hilarious now she looked back at it. She was so accustomed to nudity that she hardly noticed it any more.

And when her new mistress entered the cell, looking smart and expensive in a dark blue, buttoned down the front and belted, knee length dress, all she had to do was click her fingers and Diane went to her, naked and obedient. The woman, holding her hand down by one thigh, clicked her fingers again and Diane knew what she wanted. She moved her feet apart and felt the fingers feel their way up inside her.

"I gather the men said goodbye to you last night," she said, watching Diane's face closely. Resisting the urge to close her eyes, the better to savour the rising pleasure, Diane tried to concentrate on speech.

"Yes, Mistress," she managed, using the title easily and naturally. "They all fucked me, and some did it twice. They had one of the other girls lick me out in between, so they didn't get sloppy seconds."

The woman laughed lightly. "Well you're still pretty wet and that's good. Come on. We've got a long drive ahead of us."

She withdrew her fingers and held them up for Diane to lick and then, abruptly, she turned and left. Diane followed, mesmerised by the shapely buttocks' heft and sway beneath the tightly fitting dress.

Madam was waiting with the clothes Diane had been wearing when she arrived but her mistress waved them away.

"There's no point in the slut wearing anything. It'll just give it false hopes about its future in any case. It's better to be cruel to these creatures from the outset."

Madam smiled grimly at Diane as she absorbed the words with a sinking feeling in her stomach and a slow fire starting in her belly. When this woman used the word 'cruel', she felt, it really meant something.

There was a van parked in a yard that Diane had never been taken to before, its doors stood open and part of the flooring in the back had been removed. A long, shallow space was revealed beside the drive shaft, running from front to back and even Diane's newly aroused submissive nature couldn't stop the feeling of horror that surged through her as she took note of the shackles at each end.

Her mistress grasped her arm with thin but steely strong fingers.

"In you go!" she whispered.

Diane tried to turn and run but Sven was suddenly there, blocking her way. He picked her up by her waist, effortlessly.

"They fit in best face down. But if it struggles too much, just put it in any old way," her mistress told him.

Diane stopped struggling. The space was barely a foot deep and the thought of the boards being replaced directly onto her face was just too much. Face down was bad enough, but it could at least be tolerated.

She allowed herself to be lowered onto the cold steel plates that formed the shallow space, with her arms stretched out above her head. Her cuffs were fastened to a loop at the front end of the space. Her ankle cuffs were similarly dealt with and with no further fuss, the boarding was replaced above the back of her head.

Eventually she found the best way was to turn her face to the side, praying that there had been some air holes left as she struggled to stifle the screams that claustrophobia was forcing up her throat. The darkness seemed complete to begin with but gradually some grey light became discernible and she realised that tiny air holes had been cut in the steel. If she thought about it logically then it became clear that the woman wouldn't have parted with money for her if she was just going to suffocate her on the way.......the way to where? There had to be some sort of frontier crossing involved, hence the smuggling space, surely?

Diane wondered about calling for help when she heard someone search the van. But no sooner had she framed the thought than she felt and heard knocking above her and her new mistress called down.

"This is just to avoid the usual inconveniences one experiences in transporting naked females around. The border guards have all been well bribed, so scream all you want, it'll make no difference."

She heard boxes being piled into the van above her and then the engine started and it moved off. From the very beginning it was clear that the trip was going to be agonisingly uncomfortable. The roads were pot holed and she was mercilessly thrown about, despite her confinement. Her breasts in particular suffered against the harsh steel. The reek of exhaust fumes was a constant accompaniment to the physical pain. They made several stops and Diane heard men's voices close by and even felt them walking above her on one occasion. She debated fiercely with herself about whether or not to shout for help. It seemed absurd not to. But then what if the woman were telling the truth? If she was and there was no help to be had, what would her punishment be like? She recalled Madam's solitary confinement cell well enough to understand that even a masochist can be punished terribly.

She did nothing in the end and wondered if there were other reasons apart from the fear of reprisal.

At last the van stopped again and this time the engine was switched off. Diane heard the woman get out and speak to someone in a language she didn't understand. She heard the doors open and the boxes above her being moved. Then light flooded into her tiny prison and Diane could see her mistress standing over her, a man at her side. He said something she couldn't understand but she could guess well enough at his meaning. He was looking down at a naked and helpless woman who bore the marks of a recent beating, after all.

Large male hands reached down and freed her, then lifted her up and set her down in the open air. Diane looked around her. They were high up in some mountain range or other. Giant peaks soared high above them and seemingly endless forests carpeted the slopes until rocks and even some snow still lying in the summer took their place. At the roadside was a stone built hovel with a sign that spelled out a word she couldn't read but didn't need to. The plain wooden barrier across the road told her clearly enough that this was a frontier; a very remote one.

Diane's new owner came to stand in front of her.

"You've been a good little slut so far and we're nearly at the end of the journey. But there's one formality still to be gone through. You see up here the guards don't appreciate financial incentives, so I pay them in a different coin."

Diane understood that her naked and defenceless body was the bribe and she looked at the men standing around her. There were about ten of them, they all wore dirty and ragged uniforms, they all sported rough beards and grinned at her, showing stained and uneven teeth. The only clean things about them were their guns.

Her owner said something to them and walked off towards the cottage. Two of the men grabbed Diane and pushed her towards it as well.

Another man came out of the house and set up a table and folding chair, then he hurried back and came out again with a bottle and glass.

Diane watched as the woman fastidiously dusted the chair with a handkerchief and sat down, crossing her elegant legs.

"Let them do whatever they want to with you. It can be quite dangerous to be difficult."

This was obviously a well established routine and Diane wondered how many other slaves had passed into the hovel. A small and terrified part of her asked whether they had all come out.

She was marched into a dim interior that stank of unwashed bodies and as her eyes grew accustomed to the light she could make out about another five men. After the activities of the night before, Diane realised she was going to be one very sore girl by the time they had all played with her to their hearts' content. Once she was inside, someone slammed the door and the men began to undress. Diane knew there was no escape but couldn't help backing up to a wall and whimpering in despair. Back at Madam's she knew she had learned to enjoy cruelty but there had been some limits to it. She had known that she had value – even if it was purely financial – so no one was going to harm her. Here she was among total strangers, and dangerously armed ones at that. Somehow her new owner didn't seem to be the type to bother about the loss of a slave here or there. She probably built it into her business plan.

Diane made up her mind to do whatever it took to make sure she walked out of there.

When the men were all naked, one of them placed a bottle on the table and began pouring drinks. Diane had never seen so many cocks in one place before and it brought some relief to her terror. At least getting gangbanged was a familiar experience.

Someone pushed her towards the table and someone else's hands reached for her breasts. At her back she felt the hardness of an erect cock and as she looked down to watch the dark skinned hands with dirt encrusted in the fingernails, maul and squeeze her soft, pale breastflesh, she at last felt the first faint stirrings of lust. Another hand reached between her legs and she parted her thighs more widely. Hard, rough fingers dug into her cunt.

She felt herself moisten helplessly, the man feeling her said something and there was general laughter.

Diane didn't need a phrase book to interpret. Suddenly she was pushed hard in the back and it was clear that they wanted her bent across the table. Gingerly she lowered her chest towards the stained tabletop and grimaced as she felt her nipples squashed down into the drink-puddled and ash-spattered wood. Behind her some kind of argument broke out and she was jostled roughly. It seemed that a sort of queue was forming and when a hand descended heavily on the back of her head, forcing her face down into the mess and she felt the broad head of a cock begin to force its way into her, she assumed that an order had been decided on.

At first she was almost disappointed. These men seemed very easily satisfied, all they wanted was a quick poke and the first seven or eight finished with her before she had properly registered their presence. She certainly didn't get anywhere near a climax herself. But once their initial thirst for a woman had been slaked, they began to get more ambitious.

A hand grabbed her hair and pulled her further over the table towards a cock that was re-erect and glistening with discharge. Behind her there was a roar of protest as the man fucking her felt her being dragged away from him. But after a couple of angry exchanges she felt the man behind her lean farther over her and the cock in front of her was rammed towards her mouth. Without thinking she opened wide and furled her lips over her teeth, accepting a man's right to use whichever of her holes he chose. She knew what she had become.

It was the foulest cock she had ever tasted and her nose was rubbed against the wiry pubic hair at its base which smelled appalling. The man in her cunt finished and his place was taken by another who started energetically hammering into her, making her jerk back and forth on the cock in her mouth. The good news was that this speeded up its ejaculation which was the bitterest tasting she had ever had. The bad news was that its place was taken by another who tasted and smelled just as bad.

Someone gathered her hands together and pinned them behind her so he could lift her up enough to feel her breasts, and this helped her cope with the horrible tastes she was getting. And as she swallowed the second load of spunk the lances of pleasure from her nipples made her aware that she must be presenting a picture of dissolute sluttishness. And the fouler the cocks were that were using her, the better the slut she was proving herself to be. Mistress would be proud of her. She began to gobble greedily at every cock that waved in front of her face, sometimes even managing two at a time, nodding her head frantically to encourage them to spend so she could service the next ones. Gradually the use of her cunt slowed while the number of cocks presented for her mouth increased. Then someone started beating her bottom with a heavy belt, or so it seemed to her. The blows made her jerk as her buttock cheeks rippled and swayed and the men in front of her face cheered their comrade on. Then someone started beating her back as her arms were held out to her sides, and as she grabbed a breath, choking out thick strings of sperm onto her chin, before yet another cock claimed her, she realised she was going to come at last.

She screamed her release under a hail of lashes but her screams were muffled by the careless presence of a cock pushing for the depths of her throat and she made no attempt to swallow its spend, letting it flood out of her lips and up her nose. She lay, totally wasted, on the table. Only the hands gripping her hair keeping her from sliding off. For a blessed moment there was a lull in the queue at her face and the arse beating stopped, although the one across her back continued, pounding out a tattoo of hot, delicious pain. She groaned in appreciation of the fact that one man seemed to know she needed more.

But he was not alone. She felt a hand plunge into her molten cunt and squirm around only to withdraw cruelly fast and instead wet, sticky fingers plunged into her backside.

The men at Madam's had opened her virgin hole by the simple expedient of using it until it was able to accept them without causing them too much discomfort. Diane found it the hardest thing of all. Her sphincters had put up stout resistance and even with lube she had screamed each time as they had been wrenched apart. And even once the entry was over, she didn't care for the contrary feelings having something as big as an erect man moving backwards and forwards inside her rectum. She wanted to empty herself at the same time as something that felt like a telegraph pole was thrusting up into her. However, she did accept that if she was going to be a slut, she might as well be a proper all-three-holes one. So she tried to relax and learn to enjoy it when someone wanted to use her in that way.

Here, however, once they had given her rectum a good dose of secretion and sperm, they simply drove into her. It didn't bother them at all that she yelled as she was stretched and then plundered. She heard them happily laughing and drinking as she groaned and cried out. Despite all the times she was ejaculated into, her sphincters just weren't lubricated enough and withdrawal hurt just as much as entry because every man who took her was in a hurry to make way for his mates and didn't wait to soften inside her.

Diane was sure she would be damaged and by the time they had had their fill of her backside she was sobbing openly. They left her for a while and then they turned her onto her back.

They also lifted her bodily onto a smaller table so that her head could hang over one edge while her cunt was comfortably presented at the other. Someone beat her tits while she was being used at both ends and orgasm after orgasm ripped through her.

When it was over at last, someone rolled her off the table onto the floor and prodded her in the ribs with a toe, indicating she could go. Slowly she made it onto hands and knees and crawled gratefully for the door as the men dressed. Even when she was outside she continued to crawl, walking just wasn't an option. She was burning and sore over what felt like every square inch of her body surface and all three of her inner passages were raw as well. Her face and genitals were crusted in sperm which also matted her hair. The only parts of her which weren't caked in it were the places where it had been whipped off.

But mentally Diane was proud and calm. She had taken them all.

Beside her the elegantly shod foot of her mistress came into view, keeping pace with her slow crawl.

"You know, I've just been on the phone to someone who might be very interested in you. And I think if she could see you now, you'd interest her even more."

Diane was too exhausted to do anything other than keep crawling and hope the van wasn't far. She had taken all of them on and come through it. Her mind fastened on the word 'come'. She had never dreamed of such intensity of experience. She was a slut and she adored doing all that that meant. And now that those men had finished with her so there was no point in hanging around, she had to go on and find the next experience. Somewhere there would be others who would demonstrate her worthlessness to her – and oddly enough that very humiliation would make her feel completely at ease with herself. She just hoped it wouldn't be too long before she took another pounding like that one.

Above her she heard her Mistress's phone take a picture and then the van, its doors open came into view and she crawled into the blessed shade of the interior. She had obviously done well because she was allowed to huddle in a corner rather than be forced back into the steel case she had been brought in. The doors were slammed and the van bumped off.

She woke when they were opened again and a finger click summoned her outside. She managed to make it on her feet this time and found herself on a gravel sweep before a large house with shutters at the windows, surrounded by parkland. The mountains loomed in the distance. A man stood before her holding a collar and lead.

"There was another platoon from somewhere or other, so it got a double seeing-to," her mistress told him.

"It seems to have taken it well enough," he said, examining Diane critically.

They both laughed and then another finger click put her back on hands and knees and the collar was fastened around her neck, replacing the one she had left at Madam's, then the lead was pulled and with the gravel adding to her pains she crawled after the man and her mistress, who, it now appeared was intent on selling her on.

Slut, slut, slut – the word echoed round her brain. She loved it. She was so utterly sluttish that she could be fucked, buggered and beaten by anyone who wanted to and could be bought and sold on a whim.

They talked as they led her slowly across the gravel, it crunched beneath their shoes and dug sharply into her knees but at last they reached some concrete, which came as a blessed relief.

They stopped for a moment and the man put his foot on the back of her head, forcing her face down and leaving her backside raised, again she turned her face sideways, the man's shoe pressing hard on her cheek. Diane felt his hands part her buttocks as he leaned over her and she presumed he was inspecting the wear and tear the border guards had inflicted on her.

"It did get quite a seeing-to, didn't it?" he concluded eventually. "Better hold the viewing till it's less raw?"

"No, the sooner the better. Where it's going it'll need to be tough so a good crop of welts and a battered arse are all to the good."

"You want to mark it? Then I'll clean it up and stable it for the night."

"Yes, you can take your foot off it. It knows its place."

Diane felt a surge of pride at the compliment as the shoe was lifted away, then she saw her mistress' feet appear in front of her eyes, she watched, curious to know what was in store for her, but entirely unafraid. The woman spread her feet wider apart and from above came the sounds of material being rearranged then a shadow fell across her and she realised that her mistress was squatting over her.

Squinting sideways above her, Diane just managed to catch a glimpse of her cunt between her stockinged thighs as they descended towards her, her skirt bunched up around her hips. She came so low that for a divine second Diane's cheek was brushed by the soft sexflesh but then it lifted away and her Mistress let loose a golden stream that drummed and splashed all over her head and face. It was bitter and acidic on her eagerly questing tongue but strangely fragrant too, and so deliciously arousing! Her mistress was marking her as her property, even if it was only going to be temporary. As the golden liquid poured across her, making her eyes sting if she tried to open them but finding its way into her nose and mouth, Diane knew that despite any laws that might exist outlawing slavery, they were irrelevant in her case. She was not only in thrall to anyone who paid for her, she was an abject slave to slavery itself. She was a whore, a slut, a slave; a girl who revelled in being used and cast aside; just a body to be beaten and abused if it pleased anyone to. Her own pleasure in her use was of no concern to her users.

Her Mistress stood up and Diane stayed where she was, urine now dripping off her to add to the caked sperm. Her lead was jerked and she pushed herself up onto her hands again to crawl into the shade of what looked like a stable or a barn. There were bales of straw here and there and stalls all along one wall. At another jerk on her lead she halted and waited patiently as the man, whistling softly, moved around making some preparations. Eventually, over her head she heard the sound of an electric motor and felt ropes brush her back. The man's hands began to work at her ankles, but she was too well trained to try and see what he was doing. It was none of her business.

He stood up and walked away. The motor started again and very soon she felt an irresistible tugging at her ankles, lifting them swiftly up into the air. She couldn't help giving a terrified squeal as her hands took her weight for a few seconds and then the pull on her ankles swept her up into the air to dangle helplessly. She was used to the tremendous tension that suspension put on her ankles, at Madam's she had frequently been hung upside down in a frame, but to be swept up so dramatically and so abruptly was a new sensation entirely. As she swung, her arms hanging uselessly towards the floor, her soaked hair tangling over her face she nevertheless managed to shake it away long enough to look around. The man was standing by a wall holding a large yellow box with a panel of buttons on it and it was connected to a flexible, rubber encased cable. He grinned at her and took his thumb off a button. She stopped rising and just hung, her legs spread wide and her whole body available to him.

He strolled forwards and took hold of a breast which was almost at his head height.

"Nice tits," he said, squeezing and twisting it but ignoring the nipple itself, which in obedience to her masochism, hardened in excitement at his casual attentions.

"Hope I'll get to do more than just clean you up before you leave here – but for now......" He left her and went back to the wall where he took up a hose pipe.

Diane knew perfectly well what was coming and did her best to prepare for the shock of the freezing water that slammed into her, flattening her breasts, numbing her burning crotch and anus, blasting away the encrusted sperm. After a few minutes he stopped and soaped her up with a sponge, making sure he parted her labia and buttocks to clean her entrances. Then it was the hose again until she was shivering and swinging on her ropes. She was aching from the strain and her dangling arms hurt almost as much as her legs when he finally let her down and helped her to stand. Then he towelled her down and dried her hair. She was too tired to make any protest and in any case the feeling of being clean was delightful and to be handled with such competent ease as though she was some animal incapable of grooming herself was deeply erotic to her.

When he led her to a stall and it became clear that this was where she was to sleep, Diane felt nothing but eager curiosity. Her bed was simply a sheet over some straw. Her wrist cuffs were clipped together around the steel of a ring set in the wall at the head of the makeshift bed and a rough blanket was spread over her. Then he left her, the door closing behind him plunging the barn into comforting darkness. She fell into a deep, contented sleep immediately.

CHAPTER 7

Amelia prowled around the holding cell impatiently. She was kept naked with her hands clipped together behind her back at all times. Even meals were spoon fed to them by their guards and the men even stood over them as they used the buckets in their cells and made sure they were clean afterwards. Of course she was quite well aware that an arena slave was considered merely a creature and had no hands and no right to touch herself outside of the arena, but she hadn't realised how devastating an impact those assumptions would make when applied to her. She felt utterly mastered and so completely subjugated that it astonished her. The guards controlled every single aspect of her body and her life. If they fancied using any of the slaves to relieve sexual tensions, then it was done with the minimum of fuss. The slave concerned was simply bent over – if her vagina or rectum was required – and taken. If her mouth was needed then her lead was jerked downwards to make her kneel and she offered her mouth as a receptacle for the man's sperm.

Amelia loved it and only exhibited any disobedience when she felt it was advisable to maintain her cover as a novice. The floggings she received were competent and hard but clearly planned not to mark the merchandise too heavily. She appreciated the professionalism of the outfit and wanted to move on quickly but there were others in the batch she was with who were taking longer to train.

They were being held in a windowless room. There were twenty cages in all, each occupied by an attractive female, like her, naked and cuffed. The cages were back to back so that Amelia was surrounded by fellow slaves on three sides. Two narrow corridors outside the doors of the cages, but within the walls of the outer room, led to the feeding area at one end. The ceilings of the cages were iron bars just like the sides and formed the floor of the room above, so the guards walked above them and looked down to keep a constant watch on them.

Several of the girls wore inflatable ball gags. When she had first woken up in her cage, there had been some screaming and crying from nearby cages and the men had simply fitted the gags and pumped them up until the noise stopped. Each day at meal times the gags were undone and if the girls kept silent, food was provided. There were only two now left who wore the gags and even they kept silent for food but still kicked at their bars and struggled when they were used, so the gags remained.

The men rarely spoke and even when they did they used brief syllables such as one would with an animal, relying more on tone and gesture. Again, it was a technique that Amelia was well used to and she had had to struggle hard not to respond too readily.

The only aspect of her situation that unsettled her was the complete blank in her mind regarding how she had got where she was. There was simply nothing in her memory. There was the brief struggle in the car park and then waking in the cell. In between was just missing and she felt frustrated, having helped transport arena slaves in the past, she had a professional interest in how she had been brought here but it seemed as though she would just have to accept that she would never know and concentrate on her future. Now she was cast adrift on the brutal seas of the arenas, her greatest fear was that she might be recognised by someone and accused of spying for CSL. To ensure that she blended in she was sometimes slower to obey than she wanted to be and had on one occasion courted serious punishment by balking point blank at an order to leave her cage for exercise one afternoon. There was a small yard outside around which they were encouraged to run by a heavy strap across their rumps and thighs.

"C'mon! Out! Here girl!" the guard had barked at her clicking his fingers imperiously. She had drawn a deep breath and imitated one of the other girls who had protested the previous day.

"I'm a human being, you bastard! Talk to me properly! I demand that you…"

She hadn't got any further. The man, a tall, bearded ruffian, strode into her cell and slammed his hand across her mouth, then picked her up effortlessly and carried her out. Ordinarily slowness to obey was punished on the spot, short straps being used on the girl immediately or sometimes after she was tied to the bars of her cage. Amelia suspected that she was in for some serious punishment this time. She was taken to a room where there was only one item of furniture, a wooden St Andrew's cross set in a rectangular frame with a pivot at its centre so that it could be turned full circle. She had been put on plenty of them at The Lodge and fondly recalled Patti shafting her on one during her final visit. She loved them, but on this occasion she had to disguise her true feelings and screamed and kicked and bit until the man dropped her and shouted for help.

It took three men eventually to strap her facing the cross and even then they had a struggle to pinch her jaws hard enough to get her to open for a gag. By the time the flogging began, Amelia was well pleased with herself. The men were furious with her disobedience and two of them laid into her with single tail whips, taking it in turns to lash her from shoulders to knees. Through the gag she howled and yelled as best she could. It sounded authentic but was actually covering up her orgasms.

It was a thorough thrashing that didn't cease until even she had been driven hard and her head was lolling on one shoulder, the pain of each lash blending into the one huge pain that engulfed her and burned most brightly in her belly. When at last the lashes stopped falling, they tipped the cross forwards so that she lay parallel to the floor at the level of the men's groins, her legs spread wide and her treacherous cunt on full display. Muzzily she worried that they would find her too turned on for a novice after such a beating, but fortunately the struggle and the whipping had excited them to the extent that they simply pulled out their cocks and rammed straight into her, one after the other. Amelia took them with her head hanging down between her spread arms, groaning through the gag, appreciative of a harder flogging than she had had in a long time.

When they had finished with her they turned the cross further until she hung head down with her spread legs right in front of the men. As soon as they produced the heavy tailed flogger and showed it to her, she screamed through the gag and shook her head furiously.

To no avail. Each of them gave her ten hard, relentless lashes to the inner thighs and her engorged labia. There was no pretence in her screams then. This was what she had wanted! To be driven to her limits again. She and Brian had grown too comfortably familiar. She needed this edge, this danger. Her screams were genuinely of pain but fortunately the juice of her excitement at being made to suffer so much was disguised by the men's earlier emissions.

When they finally took her down, two of them had to support her under her armpits.

"No more lip, bitch!" the third one said, yanking her hair violently to get her to face him. Exhausted and dazed, Amelia nodded fervently and they carried her back, throwing her onto the floor of her cage contemptuously. It took her two days of exemplary obedience to get the gag removed and since then she had been the perfectly cowed little slavegirl. But that had all been about a fortnight previously as far as she could tell and she was worried that she was getting out of condition. She needn't have worried.

Once the gags finally came off the most rebellious captives, the guards started a gym routine in another part of the building. The slaves were shackled to various treadmills, rowing machines and weight lifting devices. Under the whips they were driven to the point of collapse and their performances noted. From then on there were regular sessions and it wasn't lost on any of the girls that the men with the whips now knew what they were capable of; there was no slacking.

Amelia was filled with excitement every time she was shackled to a machine; she knew perfectly well what she was being honed for and couldn't wait. She ran on the treadmill till sweat blinded her, her breasts bouncing and frequently being fondled by one or other of the guards, sometimes they even nipple clamped them for fun.

Every now and then she would make a whimpered protest if one of the men wanted to take her, just for appearances' sake but her moist eagerness down below was now taken as the result of good training and caused no comment.

And then at long last the day came.

The whip handles and riding crops were run along the bars of the cages as usual and the girls struggled blearily out of the low, narrow beds as usual. And as usual the four guards who woke them made their choice. Amelia was one of them and was jerked by her lead down to her knees. The guard who wanted her was the one who had seen to her worst beating and she was keen to taste him again, he had frequently made use of her subsequent to that thrashing and had sometimes beaten her purely for his pleasure. He was her type of man. He pulled out his impressive cock in front of her face, it was already hard and thick, rearing up eagerly from his belly, he stroked the foreskin back from the broad, shiny helm and allowed her lips to slip over it and her mouth to receive him. He tasted clean and fresh for once and Amelia set about obtaining a good mouthful of breakfast sperm, nodding her head vigorously and sinking down on him until she felt his thickness fill her throat.

He sighed in pleasure above her and then the day's routine began to change.

"I'll miss you after today," he said. "You'll fetch good money with a mouth like that and you're fit too. Hope you can stay the course in the arenas." Then he grabbed her head, just as she was absorbing the impact of words actually addressed to her, and began to pump himself into her. For a few seconds her world contracted to feeling the huge thing she was just about able to close her lips around, flexing and jumping madly in her mouth as it spurted three, four, five times and then jerked less strongly as it released some final thick splashes into her throat and she struggled to get them down smoothly. It was today then!

There was no spoon-fed breakfast that day, just blessedly hot showers for the first time and the men stripped off and joined the girls under the torrents, soaping them down, enjoying themselves and relaxing for once, fucking whichever of the girls they chose as often as they liked. Amelia was bent forward on several occasions and taken while hot water drummed on her back and flowed around her face and the cock inside her battered her to orgasm. The constant state of helplessness in which she was kept had really worked wonders, she realised as she bent over for the fourth time and felt a finger work into her bottom.

It was second nature to her now to respect the men who fed her, cleaned her and controlled her. She depended utterly on them and it was only fair that if her body gave them pleasure, they should use it. The finger in her bottom was joined by another that clearly had some lube on it and once three fingers had stretched her enough they were replaced by the thick helm of a cock. She humped her back and spread her legs wider as the intruder nosed into her body, wrenching her sphincters to their limit. She grinned at the pain and welcomed the opportunity to suffer for a man's pleasure. He pushed hard and held her hips, sliding further in and rubbing her inner tissues in the familiar, strange way. She pressed back as he lunged again and then braced herself to remain as still as she could while he moved back and forth in her tightest channel. She was nowhere near an orgasm by the time he spent himself in her innards but enjoyed the obvious pleasure it gave him.

They were all towelled dry and then some girls appeared. And they wore clothes. The novelty made Amelia stare at them as though they were aliens, and in some senses they were. They wore jeans and brightly coloured tops and as far as Amelia could see they were a type of groom and chatted happily while they dried the slaves' hair and brushed it until each of them looked quite glamorous in their nudity. They even had some makeup applied, though Amelia felt hers was put on far too heavily.

As she sat, silent and unmoving on the edge of her bed, while her groom fussed around her and chatted with the other grooms in the surrounding cages, Amelia experienced an odd sense of perspective about her previous life. She recalled how she, Anna Marie, Helga and Raika had so often tended to the CSL slaves while they talked about which man had had them the night before and what he – or they – had done to them, just as these girls were. Meanwhile the slaves had sat, calm and mute, just as she was doing now; apart and remote, and somehow above these chattering, flighty little things who didn't understand the true nature of complete submission the way she and the other slaves had been made to. Although the grooms, like the guards, spoke in English, flavoured with a wide variety of accents, it felt as though they were talking a foreign language.

Even as she squatted over the bucket in the corner of her cage and relieved herself, her lead held casually by her groom who then wiped her clean, Amelia felt that a slave's life held depths that some females would never appreciate. And strangely she felt that the deeper she sank, in the view of air heads like these grooms, the higher she soared in a weirdly inverted world that only a slave could understand.

The guards reappeared as the grooms led their charges out of the cages and the procession was carefully shepherded along many corridors and up several flights of stairs. Amelia noted that each guard now carried a sort of stun gun at his belt. She almost smiled at the thought that whoever ran this operation had no idea of how thorough their own training had been. She looked at her leashed and collared fellows and saw only a calm acceptance of their fate in each face. Besides, where on earth was a naked and collared female likely to run to?

Eventually they came to a long, bare room with a plain wooden floor. The ceiling was high and one wall featured large, tinted glass windows. Amelia could see a cityscape through them. They were high up amongst other tall buildings but skyscrapers towered far above them even so. It could have been any modern city in any part of the world.

The sound of the grooms' high heels and the men's shoes echoed as the procession entered. Down the centre of the room ran two long, thick steel poles, the top one about five feet above the lower one. At each end and in the middle, they were mounted in heavy wooden, vertical stakes bolted to the floor. Each steel pole had many sets of leather straps riveted to it. Amelia's heart leapt into her mouth as she took it all in. She recognised an auction room when she saw one. At last she was moving on.

Each slave was mounted with her arms spread out along the top bar, the leather straps wound repeatedly around the forearms before being tied off. Their feet couldn't touch the lower bar and so their bodies hung slanting backwards slightly until their ankles were dragged forwards and stretched down so that their cuffs could be tied to more straps. She was not in the least surprised that they were also dragged well apart. A prospective owner would most certainly want to explore a slave's cunt, after all.

All along the line, strained gasps and moans escaped the slaves as the full tension of their restraint took effect. Amelia herself bit her lip as the strain on her shoulders began to tell but the man attending to her twisted one nipple so harshly that she yelped and he rammed a gagging strap into her mouth, which he then tied off around the bar behind her, dragging her head back until she was staring at the ceiling. Her mouth was filled with the taste of leather but at least she could bite hard into it to help deal with the discomfort.

The following hours were a strange blend of excitement, boredom and pain. Soon after she had been mounted, she heard the doors they had entered by thrown open and a crowd of people enter. Mainly she heard male voices but there were one or two women present as well. She heard them spread out along the row of slaves and caught snatches of conversation.

"Legs too short for running but looks sturdy enough for log pulling........Looks like she could handle herself in a ring........cunt's wet! That's always a good sign!..........Tits too big...........We don't need any more runners, we need tough whip fodder.......... Christ! Look at the nipples on this one!"

It was hauntingly familiar. She had heard Brian and Carlo argue and comment almost identically in the evenings at The Lodge as they browsed online, and at the auction she had so recently attended with them. At the thought of them, her heart skipped a beat. Part of the reason she had put her plan into action when she had, was that she knew that CSL was fully stocked with slaves currently and it would mean that neither Brian nor Carlo would be attending auctions. Nevertheless she couldn't help listening for their voices, terrified of being identified before she could be bought by a stable. But nowhere was there Carlo's Spanish accented voice or Brian's deep tones and she gradually relaxed.

It helped that hands were exploring her almost constantly. Her breasts and up-tilted nipples were stroked and gripped and twisted. Her thighs and buttocks were squeezed and inevitably fingers were inserted into her vagina. With her head tipped back so far, she couldn't see the faces of the people who were helping themselves to her body. But being so tightly restrained and helpless lent a strange kind of excitement and intensity to the feeling of being molested. She knew that her cunt was flooding in response to being entered so often, most people simply wiped her juice off on her stomach when they had finished with her. The snaps of surgical gloves being fitted increasingly echoed around the room and Amelia soon felt slick fingers working their way into her anus from behind her. Even through the gagging straps, some of the slaves were squealing in protest and Amelia felt nothing but contempt for them. They would probably not sell if they put up too much resistance and would miss out on the thrill of the arenas.

"Lot number eight. This one's interesting."

It was a woman's voice coming from just in front of her and Amelia immediately focussed on it; hoping they were talking about her, she had felt a number being stencilled onto her lower stomach but as it had been done after her head had been wrenched back, she hadn't been able to see it. A cool hand stroked her left breast and fingers rolled her achingly hard nipple.

"Pretty tits......and not too big either," the woman said.

A man snorted. "Value for money does not reside in the prettiness of the creature's tits!" he said. "We need good all round ability."

"I know, Eric! But she's got to earn her keep outside the arena as well as in it and an attractive pair of tits to beat or stick things in will draw the punters. Besides, the thighs are really quite strong," the woman replied.

Amelia felt the hand leave her breast and instead she felt fingers begin to knead her thighs. A man's hands joined them and soon his fingers squirmed into her cunt, stretching it and rummaging their way as far into her as they could go. The arrogance of their intrusion made Amelia go weak with pleasure. But all too soon they were withdrawn and she felt the smaller fingers of a woman wriggling their way into her, she had sharp nails and Amelia winced once or twice as they scratched her tender inner tissues. They spent a longer time inside her and as they withdrew, they played with her clitoris. It was the first time anyone had bothered with it, it didn't affect her athleticism so it wasn't important. But this woman was knowingly rubbing at her and Amelia moaned in delight as sharp tingles of excitement played havoc with her innards and her nipples throbbed into even harder erection.

"It's enjoying itself," the woman said. "That's good. Masochism always helps in the arena."

Amelia gurgled into her strap as the pleasure mounted and then she twisted in her bonds out of shock as the man began to probe her bottom.

"Its arse has been well enough opened up," he told the woman.

"Of course. They know their business here," she replied. "Make a note and we'll see how she moves around the ring at the bidding."

And with that they were gone, leaving Amelia distraught and on the very edge of orgasm. But even in the midst of her misery as the discomfort made itself felt all the more and the pleasure waned, in her mind Amelia was exultant. She had made an impression! Someone might bid for her! She might be only a few minutes away from being a fully owned, bought-and-paid-for completely anonymous slave.

She played the incident back in her mind over and over as more hands felt and pawed at her and more voices discussed her – some quite enthusiastically. But it was the woman's voice that stuck in Amelia's mind. It was cool and knowledgeable, and she could imagine it being wonderfully cruel if the mood was right. It was the voice of someone she could serve.

Her groans of relief joined with others as she was finally released and lifted down. However her hands were immediately denied her once more as her wrists were clipped together behind her back. She had to wait her turn for a guard to come and rub life back into her limbs, then they were led around on their leashes for a while to ease the aches and pains of long restraint and to make sure they were all walking well. Amelia made sure she kept her shoulders back and her head up, desperate to please the woman who had expressed an interest in her.

The only concession made to their femininity before they were sold was that their hair was brushed once more, their make up was checked and repaired if necessary and they were given four inch heeled court shoes to wear. They were led around once more and encouraged to put a catwalk sway into their gait.

"Any bitch doesn't sell, she'll come back for remedial training!" one guard yelled at them and immediately shapely buttocks began to sway as hips were swung, heads came up and breasts were pushed out. The guard in question had his stun gun out in one hand and a long single tail whip in the other.

Each lot was called out in ascending order so Amelia had plenty of time to fret but eventually she was called and her groom tugged a strand of hair into place, smoothed and patted it one last time and then pulled on her leash.

"C'mon girl," she urged, clicking her fingers and with her heart hammering in her chest – terrified of not being sold – Amelia followed her out of the viewing room and into the auction ring.

CHAPTER 8

Diane shivered slightly in the chilly breeze that still blew despite the bright sunshine at this altitude.

Her Mistress tutted and smacked her bottom hard.

"Stand still!" she ordered. "We've only got two days to get you ready."

She was standing naked on the lawn behind the house she had been brought to only the night before. She had been allowed to sleep until quite late and had awoken refreshed and alert, but still hurting at vagina and anus.

To her amazement the man who had cleaned her and put her to sleep, fed her breakfast from a bowl as she knelt up in her stall, her hands still clipped to the steel ring in the wall. He had encouraged her to eat with little phrases and noises – pleased ones when she took a good mouthful of the porage-like cereal and annoyed ones when she managed to spill a bit on her chin, taking it off the spoon. She realised that this was simply another way of carrying on their habit of treating her as an 'it' and she had to admit that being kept in a barn made it all seem almost natural. Clearly being a slut wasn't enough, she had to learn how not to be human as well if she wanted to please her owners.

Pleasantly intrigued as to how the day would shape up, she watched the man stand up when he had finished feeding her and she saw a very interesting bulge in the crotch of his jeans. Immediately she spread her thighs and thrust her breasts forwards. He laughed.

"Horny little bitch, aren't you?" he said and reached down to pat her hair. Then he released her wrists from the ring but then clipped them behind her back before helping her to her feet and leading her out into the main part of the barn. There he released her wrists again and had her go onto all fours, then hoisted her up for hosing down again. And it was while she was swinging and gasping in the wake of the water that her Mistress entered, looking as cool and chic as ever, an elegant scarf around the neck of a tailored blouse which was tucked into the waistband of full cut, knee length skirt, her feet were once again shod in to-die-for hand made court shoes. She carried a riding crop, Diane couldn't help noticing.

The man ignored her and carried on with what he had been doing, which was to examine her vagina and then to open her anus.

"Well?" the woman asked.

"It's mended pretty well. No lasting damage but you can see where it's been well shagged and buggered," he replied.

"Good. She's coming the day after tomorrow, so we'd better put it through its paces and see if it can grasp basic training."

"I still think it's too lightly built for her purposes. Some of the stables have got real bruisers nowadays."

"Yes but there's still room for all round performers. Get it out here and I'll show you."

Diane had no idea what to make of the conversation but determined to play the role they seemed to want her to and be as animal-like as possible.

Once she was back on her feet and the dizziness of upside down suspension had passed, she was led out on her leash and taken to a huge expanse of beautifully mown lawn behind the house.

Her Mistress was waiting with a pile of leather and metal at her feet that meant nothing at all to Diane but she couldn't help looking at her superbly turned out Mistress running a strap between her elegantly manicured fingers, and regretted her own nudity. Too late she realised that not only was that a lapse in her thinking – why should she require clothes after all? – but that also she had looked at someone who was her superior.

Of course, her Mistress had seen it and dropping the strap, reached out one hand and lifted her chin. Diane, now chastened kept her eyes down but even so was able to see the other hand lift back, ready to strike. She tensed and suddenly the side of her face exploded into pain with a deafening smack as the hand landed. She staggered sideways and only a savage tug on her leash brought her back to standing.

She shook her head to try and clear it but then her Mistress' hand was back at her chin and Diane's lower lip trembled as she realised she was in for another numbing slap.

If anything the second one was harder and despite an almost choking tug on her leash, she went down to her knees, dazed and blinded for a second.

"That should remind it of its place," her Mistress said. "Now get it up and I'll show you why I bought it."

Diane felt a new pain explode across her left hip and realised the riding crop had been used. She scrambled unsteadily to her feet and stood once again, her gaze fixed firmly on the grass in front of her and the feet of the man and woman who now controlled her.

She felt her Mistress' hands on her shoulders and neck.

"Look. See how the muscle here is well developed and the head sits well – neck not too long."

The hands moved and touched her chin. Instinctively she shied away and took another slash from the crop as the leash pulled her back.

Again the hands took hold of her chin, turning her face from side to side.

"Not bad looking, strong jaw. It'll need that in the pens. Anything goes in there these days." Again it was the woman speaking and again, Diane had no idea what they were talking about.

"Look at the depth of the rib cage." The examination moved down her body and hands touched the sides of her chest. "Good lung expansion; I bet once it's used to its harness it'll run all day if needed. But these are what clinched it for me."

Diane, still carefully looking down, saw both the man and the woman squat in front of her.

Her Mistress put her hands round her left thigh.

"Feel the tone of that," she invited the man and he did the same with her right thigh, whistling with appreciation after a few seconds.

"I see what you mean," he said.

"Put that together with the lung capacity and I reckon you've got a good fighter and runner. Plus of course, it's got great tits, takes the whip well and can be fucked and buggered until the cows come home."

Diane almost moaned aloud at the erotic jolt such a judgement, given in such coarse words, delivered to her belly.

"Let's get it tacked up," the man suggested. "And get it broken to a bit."

Diane still had no idea what they were talking about but it was true that in her previous life, while her job had mainly kept her desk bound, she had compensated for it by running on the heath near her flat and by working out regularly. She had told the woman all that during the long beating at Madam's place.

They began to rummage about in the pile of strapping and Diane shifted her feet impatiently as the breeze stung her skin into goose pimpling.

"Stand still! We've only got two days to get you ready!"

Ready for what? How did running and 'pens'- whatever they were – have anything to do with being a sex slave?

Half an hour later she knew – at least she knew part of what the 'running' was about.

Her back teeth were clenched on a cold steel bit that ran through her mouth, it tasted horrible but had been rammed hard in so that her lips were stretched into an unnatural grimace. Her face and head were encased in a web of thin straps that supported heavy blinkers and reins that connected to the rings at either end of the bit. She was bridled and harnessed as a pony. But as a human pony, there were further humiliations that Diane had never dreamed of. Her breasts were circled at their roots by slender leather straps that joined her two inch deep collar and limited the amount of sway and wobble that running caused. Her nipples throbbed in the grips of clamps that had small bells attached but worst of all was below her waist. A leather belt was cinched tight at the waist itself and a further strap ran down her front, bisected her labia and supported a dildo that shifted and rubbed maddeningly inside her as she ran. After the ordeal of the previous day, it had taken several hard swipes of the crop to get her to open her legs wide enough to fit the thing but once she had given in, a few seconds' fingering by the man had her wet enough to take it. But the butt plug had been pure hell. She had had to bend over, harnessed and tacked up while humiliation was poured on humiliation as her Mistress worked huge amounts of lube into her still-stinging anus. She had wept and cried as they had eventually forced the steel thing into her and when finally she had been able to stand up, by craning her head round she had seen that an upward curving rod came off the base of the plug and sprouted a genuine horse hair tail that swept the backs of her thighs.

She had groaned and blinked her tear-blurred eyes, astonished at the depths of degradation which had existed outside her knowledge all her life.

Her Mistress had stood in front of her and slapped her breasts sharply, telling her to buck up and settle down but Diane had not been able to stem the tears. She could have enjoyed being beaten and abused, but this relentless and methodical humiliation drove her into despair.

"It'll never make it," the man had opined.

"Nonsense!" her Mistress had snorted. "It just needs breaking. Bring it round to the front of the house and wait for me there."

She had snapped the clamps onto her nipples and marched away. Diane had tried to scream but the bit had reduced her to a strangled gurgle. The clamps were wicked little things with toothed jaws. Yet more tears flooded her eyes.

The man had left her where she was, standing on the grass and had brought up a small trap that had shafts which curved gracefully inwards from the seats to where, she, the pony stood. The man had clipped her cuffs to raised, horizontal, thin bars screwed into the tops of the shafts and had then taken his place in the trap behind her, while she had gripped her fingers around the shafts. She had felt the trap shift and had experienced a slight increase in the weight of the shafts she was holding. But even while she was sniffing her tears up and determining that they would never break her into this barbarous existence, the driving whip had struck her. A spiteful length of whipcord arced over her left shoulder and stung her left breast.

"Walk on!" the man called and a second strike smacked into her right breast.

Instinctively she moved her shoulders forwards to shield herself and in so doing exerted a pull on the trap. It moved behind her and two more maddening stings across her back had her walking forwards, pulling the trap. And that was all it took, she reflected bitterly. A man who knew how to wield a whip beat her a couple of times and she sank from being a slut to being a beast of burden.

The whip hissed across her back twice more, leaving hot lines of stinging pain in its wake and Diane's masochism came to her rescue, the pain triggered pleasure in her dildo-stuffed cunt she abandoned herself to whatever was required of her.

"Trot!" the man called and lashed several more times.

With more ease than she would have thought possible, she lifted her thighs in turn and pushed off with her bare feet against the cool grass as she accelerated into a trot, the trap wagging slightly behind her as she strained. But very quickly she was up to speed and breathing normally. The whip slowed and the man made a clicking noise with his mouth. Diane took that to mean he was satisfied with her. She felt a steady pressure on her right rein and began to turn in that direction, finding that she was turning towards the house. The whip rested lightly on her right shoulder to reinforce the instruction and when the reins told her to straighten up again, it rested lightly against her hip to remind her to keep up the pace. She made it to the front door without incurring any further lashes and was rewarded by a pat on her flank from her Mistress who was waiting for them.

"See? It's hardly breathing hard at all!" she called and the man conceded that she had run well enough.

Diane, still struggling with the confusion of being treated like an animal whilst at the same time deliberately being stimulated as a woman, by means of the butt plug and the dildo stuffing her, nevertheless felt slaveish pride swell her chest at the compliment.

Her Mistress handed a small picnic hamper up to her colleague and then joined him in the trap. Diane felt the weight shift behind her again but was surprised by how little the extra person affected it. The rig had to be well balanced, she thought, as the whip once again lashed her into her work.

"We'll make a day of it, and put it through its paces. And you can try it out as well," her Mistress told the man as Diane, again with an ease that surprised and pleased her, thrust herself into a trot and set the dildo to wreaking pleasurable havoc inside her.

They worked her all morning. Running her flat out at times through the parkland. The man could play her body with the whip like a musician could play his instrument. He knew when to really lay into her to override the distractions of the plug and dildo. He knew when an agonising strike around her hip that bit at her labia would get just a bit more pace out of her than she thought she could give. He knew when a swift blizzard of lashes over her shoulders, savaging her breasts would shock her straight from a walk to a gallop.

By the time they stopped for lunch, Diane was helplessly in love with being a pony and with her driver.

She was gasping for breath and dribbling saliva onto her chin, her teeth clattering on her bit when she at last felt a hard pull back on the reins and was able to slow down from the mad gallop she had been lashed into. They were approaching a stand of tall pine trees and as she staggered to a halt she sobbed with relief as she felt her passengers alight.

The man calmly unclipped one end of the bit and took it out of her mouth, once he had released her hands from the shafts, allowing her to resume a normal expression and ease her aching lips. Meanwhile her Mistress had a hand over her heart and was counting, whilst checking her watch.

"Not bad," she said as Diane's breathing calmed. "Back to normal in only a few seconds despite a lay off while Williams trained it. I told you, given a few weeks' proper training it'll be just fine."

The man grunted non-commitally and Diane swore she would win him over somehow. He hooked a finger into one of her cheek straps and led her to stand under a branch of one of the trees, then he clipped a strap to one of her wrist cuffs, which had been clipped together behind her back immediately she was free of the trap, ran it forward between her legs and then threw it over the branch and hauled on it. Almost at once, Diane was forced almost onto tip toe as the strap cut up into her groin and ran tightly up her front, between her breasts, forcing her to tilt her head backwards as it ran up past her face. She felt the man tie it off and moaned in despair as she realised he intended to leave her like that. He merely chuckled however and unclamped her nipples. Diane gave a full blooded yell as he walked away and the blood rushed back into her long-constricted flesh. But even as she sobbed and wept while the pain washed over her, she heard relaxed laughter from behind her and the pain turned to pure erotic bliss at the thought that she was giving pleasure by suffering.

As the minutes passed, however, Diane became aware that her suffering was far more subtle than she had realised. The hobbling strap cut cruelly at her slit and pressed her crupper strap hard against her clitoris, furthermore, the man had not pulled her right onto tip toe so she was able to push herself up a little and let herself down, resulting in a delightful frisson that she felt she had earned after a hard morning's work. But she had not been given permission and Madam's training had beaten into her the wrongness of a slave pleasuring herself without permission. On the other hand if she craned her head sideways she could see that her Mistress' attention was definitely not on her presently.

The two dominants had unpacked their hamper and drunk a glass or two of wine, then had lain down together, Diane had heard her Mistress say something about watching a pony's arse cheeks wobble all morning under the whip and needing relief as a result. Now, as she furtively began to saw her clitoris against the straps she saw that the man had stripped off, revealing a wiry physique, he was now lying beside Diane's Mistress whose skirt had been rucked up to her waist and whose legs were carelessly wide spread. The man's hand was busily engaged between them, his wrist turning and flexing at her groin. Diane heard her moan in pleasure and faintly she could hear the slurping noise of a cunt that was more than ready for penetration.

The man rolled over to lie between the spread legs and Diane watched as his back humped and his feet braced themselves, then her Mistress' legs wrapped themselves round his hips and she watched him begin to fuck her. She almost wept afresh but with frustration this time. However hard she rubbed herself against the strap, she couldn't quite orgasm, the crupper strap just wouldn't let enough sensation through. Grimly she persevered though, slowly letting the wet, slapping noises and grunts from the dominants fade and even allowing herself soft moans and mews of frustration as she sawed more and more frantically, ignoring the aches in her straining feet and thighs. Then suddenly it felt as though she might make it; a fluttering deep inside her drove her on, the pleasure mounting. But suddenly a heavy hand descended on her shoulder and reached up to untie the hobble strap.

Diane groaned as she felt the pleasure subside and she realised she was in trouble as well.

"Aah! And it was doing so well!" her Mistress said from just behind her. "Well never mind, we'll use it and then punish it. Bring it over here."

Again the man, whose hand it had been on her shoulder, hooked a finger into a cheek strap and dragged her as she stumbled behind him to where the picnic had been laid out. Her Mistress was looking a little tousled but a fierce light was in her eyes as she helped push Diane down onto her back. As on the previous evening, as soon as she was down, her Mistress hitched up her skirt and squatted down onto her face. But this time she didn't pee and this time Diane's mouth was facing upwards. That was what she wanted, and Diane once again saw the woman's plump lipped cunt descend towards her. But this time there were pearls of semen still clinging to the lips and Diane knew she was in for what Madam had called a 'cocktail' – an after-fuck mouthful of cunt juice and sperm. It was nectar, and Diane eagerly foraged inside the woman, hunting with her tongue and sucking down the issue greedily, mashing her face up into the woman's pelvis as she settled on her knees and spread them to lower herself even more. Meanwhile she heard the man stand astride her and spread his own legs wide.

"Oh yes! Give me cock!" she heard her Mistress say and guessed he was going to mouth fuck her.

"Mmm!" The wordless groan confirmed her guess as her Mistress sucked the man in.

All concerns about her own pleasure fled from her mind as she found herself at the bottom of this threesome. It was where she belonged and she squirmed and wriggled, trying to bring as much pleasure as she could to the cunt that was mashing down on her. At last, by wriggling especially fiercely, and with her tongue aching and her face soaking in outpourings, she managed to tongue-lash her Mistress' clitoris and was rewarded by cock-muffled moans of delight and renewed writhing on her face.

After only a few minutes she heard the man cry out and her Mistress held still as she concentrated on swallowing then suddenly the urgency returned and Diane's face was ploughed by her Mistress as she rubbed herself to orgasm and Diane herself felt a small surge of orgasmic pleasure as the woman finally groaned and subsided sideways off her. For a long moment Diane panted and blinked in the light, licking cunt juice off her chin. Then the man loomed over her.

"It'll have to be cunt flogged for wanking without permission," he said.

"Of course. See to it, and if it comes, leave it chained in the yard for the night." Her Mistress' voice was flat and calm and Diane knew without a shadow of a doubt that she would be spending the night out of doors.

Her crupper strap was unbuckled where she lay and she gasped as the dildo was slid out, then the man lifted her ankles up until they were above her head, then her Mistress grabbed them and pulled them further so that she was bent double with her feet beyond her head, held down firmly with her thighs and cunt blatantly displayed to a craftsman with a whip. She was doomed; there was no way she wouldn't come.

Using the driving whip he laid on twenty hard lashes, working the spiteful cord across the backs of her thighs, sometimes the lash lovingly tormenting the engorged lips of her cunt from side to side, and sometimes he ran it the full length of her lips, making the tip bite at her stomach. After ten lashes he sank his hand into her flooding vagina.

"Wet as all hell!" he said.

"Give it the other ten and chain it out for the night." Her Mistress' voice betrayed no emotion at all and strangely Diane took the remaining lashes calmly and with a deeper pleasure than she had ever known before. It was simply irrelevant whether she was well behaved or not, she finally realised. She existed to be punished in one way or another by anyone whose fancy it took. She was looking forward to seeing how uncomfortable being chained out in the yard for the night might be.

She was run for a further three hours before being fed. And at long last the man who had driven and flogged her so expertly, laid her down in her stall and deigned to fuck her. With her hands clipped behind her back, she had to concentrate on using her legs and pelvis to show how much she appreciated his kindness. She bucked up under him and then wrapped her legs around him as he came and was smiling proudly as he led her outside to be chained down.

"Not a bad fuck at all," he told her Mistress as he locked her lead to a foot tall post set in concrete, while she knelt beside it. Then they spread some bits of straw around for her and left her.

It rained in the night and by the morning Diane was as happy as she could ever remember being. She was cold, shivering, dishevelled and so turned on that she came as soon as the dildo was rammed into her, ready for another day's work.

CHAPTER 9

Amelia tried to keep her gaze locked on the floor directly ahead of her and to ignore the sea of faces which surrounded the auction ring. It was in another huge room with a polished wooden floor and a circular space had been roped off in its centre.

Her lead had been handed to a big man in a white coat once the groom had taken her through the door. He walked ahead of her, loosely holding the leather loop attached to the chain that ran forwards between her legs.

As if from a great distance she heard the auctioneer's voice;

"Lot number eight, ladies and gentlemen! A specimen in her prime, I think you'll agree. Very shapely hips, good legs…."

Here the man leading her, jerked her lead upwards suddenly and made Amelia go onto tip toe.

"Note the muscle definition please! We think she has all round ability and she has responded well to basic training….."

Having posed for a moment or two in the strained position of having a chain cutting up into her soft cunt flesh to show off the sinews in her legs, Amelia was allowed to continue to walk around the ring and she turned the auctioneer's voice off as he recited how much she could bench press, how fast she could run and for how long, how many times she had been flogged – she knew the drill. Her main job now was to make herself look a million dollars and she concentrated on swaying her hips as she was led close to the rope and could almost feel the audience's breath on her shoulder. She heard some comments about her that made her heart race; someone speculating as to how well she would fuck, someone else fancying using needles on her tits.

Wherever she was bound, she knew that there would be people who would want to do that and more. She couldn't wait.

Occasionally as the auctioneer's interminable patter went on, the impassive man leading her would stop and pull her to him, then turn her to face the crowd while he squeezed his hand cruelly hard into her breastmeat and demonstrated how docile she was and how little sag there was in the breasts and how far her nipples could erect.

Once or twice Amelia dared to glance up and see if she could spot a woman who might be the one who said she might bid for her. She didn't dare look up for too long though, in case she appeared to be defiant. At last she was led to the centre of the ring and brought to a halt beside the auctioneer's dais, then the bidding got underway. It had been a part of her nightmares for months that the auctioneer would ask for bids and receive none. But now that the moment came, she needn't have worried. The bidding opened briskly and she immediately stood up straighter and more proudly as her price reached the sort of level that she knew arena slaves fetched. But it didn't stop where she thought it might. The bids kept on coming fast and big for a long time before they finally slowed and she was stunned by the amounts being bandied about, and furthermore she had no way of knowing who it was who was bidding but at last it seemed there were just two buyers and her price was simply astonishing. Her heart thundered as the auctioneer began to close on her.

"Lot number eight! Any more bids? Going...."

Amelia cast one last look around the circle of predatory faces. There was a flash of white as a catalogue was raised. Amelia's heart leapt, it seemed as if it was a woman who was holding the card and making one last bid.

The auctioneer confirmed her suspicions as he thanked 'the lady' for her bid, added another thousand to Amelia's price and then declared that she was; "Going......going.....Lot number eight, gone!"

In a daze Amelia allowed herself to be led off. For months she had felt that not only did she want the absolute submission that the arenas demanded, she needed it because she could also be a good performer. But now she at last knew that someone else agreed with her and had put their money where their mouth was to boot. Amelia swore that she would not let her new owner down.

She was taken back to her cell and a red card on the door signified that she had been sold. Impatiently she paced about, waiting to be claimed and at last lots of footsteps sounded along both corridors outside the cells as the auction came to an end. They belonged mainly to men who were claiming their purchases. Mostly the slaves were tied at the ankles as well as wrists, put in fine mesh sacks and slung over the shoulders of strong lieutenants. But Amelia's owner was different.

She was a woman in her mid forties, Amelia reckoned, with a strong, handsome face. She was grey eyed and had black hair that was just turning a little grey at the temples. She was taller than Amelia by several inches and her figure was slender but she carried herself with absolute confidence so that she dominated the cell the minute she entered it. She was accompanied by a man who appeared to be in his sixties and was slightly less tall than the woman.

"Sit down and listen to me," the woman said immediately she entered. It was the voice Amelia remembered, cool and authoritative – and cruel.

Amelia sat on the edge of the bed, looking up adoringly at the woman who now owned her.

"We can put you in a sack like the rest of the merchandise or we can give you some clothes and you can walk as far as the truck. Which do you want?"

"Oh I'll walk! I won't try and escape, you can trust me!" Amelia's voice sounded odd to her own ears, it had been weeks since she had spoken last but she was desperate to reassure this woman that she had spent her money wisely.

The woman waved her words aside however. "Eric!"

The man threw a carrier bag at her and leaned over her to free her wrists. Meanwhile the woman had taken a simple vibrator out of her bag and was offering it to Amelia.

"Put this in your cunt, my dear. It's been adapted a little. If you try to escape, I can put the same voltage right inside you as a police tazer can deliver."

Eric had upended the bag and now handed her a thong. Amelia swallowed nervously but took the vibrator, then the thong and cautiously spread her legs.

"Turn the bottom as if you're turning it on," the woman told her.

She did so with trembling fingers. Nothing happened however except the woman smiling a cold, hard smile, taking something that looked like a car's remote control locking device out of her bag.

"Put it in. Once it's inside and you make one wrong move; I'll take you down."

The thing felt cold and alien as Amelia struggled to insert it through dry lips, it chilled her insides and she had to rub her clitoris and thrust several times before she could accept it.

Then she stepped into the thong, it felt odd and cramping somehow to have a piece of cloth over genitals that had been on display for weeks. The simple shirt that she shrugged on and buttoned up also felt strangely constricting across her breasts but the short skirt she approved of, it made her legs appear longer she felt.

Eric seemed to resent the clothes.

"They're just livestock, Sadia!" he said. "It's a waste of money putting clothes on them!"

"This way we don't have to pay for hired muscle. Just two men to drive the truck and we get docile little bitches into the bargain." Again the woman smiled and to Amelia's consternation, fingered the remote control.

With no apparent restraint on her, Amelia left her cell walking between the woman and Eric. At first the guards made a move to try and grab her but Sadia explained why Amelia was going to be a good girl and they backed off, laughing and encouraging the woman to try the device out.

Outside it was raining and dark. Amelia looked around quickly just out of curiosity and saw a number of shops and advertising hoardings, the writing all seemed to be Cyrillic and she concluded that she was in Russia or one of its satellite states at least. A big truck was parked in a narrow street just a few minutes' walk away. It was bizarre to walk among normal people, knowing that she had been bought and sold and was holding a device in her cunt that could stop a charging bull, and would certainly stop *her* if her owner just moved her thumb a little to the left......

As they approached the truck from the rear, a man jumped down from the cab and met them.

"Nice looking one, Ma'am," he opined, giving Amelia the once over.

"Just get on with it, please. We've got more to pick up yet," the woman said.

He grinned and slammed up the handles that locked the doors, then opened one a little but held it. There was the sound of some movement inside. Turning just slightly towards Diane, her new owner jerked her head towards the man who climbed up into the truck while still keeping the door ajar. He reached for her hand, pulled her up and Amelia found herself standing in a meat wagon. It was transporting livestock – just as Eric had said. It was cruder than the CSL horsebox but a lot bigger. It was currently holding fifteen women, all of them chained to a solid steel bar that ran round the perimeter of the trailer about three feet above the floor. They all sat on the straw covered floor dressed similarly to her and all of them had ball gags in their mouths. Wide eyes regarded her as she looked around.

The man grabbed a riding crop from beside the door as he closed it behind Amelia.

"Get your knickers off and take out the zapper," he ordered.

It never crossed Amelia's mind to do anything other than obey him.

She lifted her skirt and pulled the thong down until she could step out of it but when she reached back up to pull out the 'zapper' the man knocked her hand away.

"Changed my mind," he said. "I fancy a handful of your cunt."

Again, it was all perfectly normal for her to allow a complete stranger access to her body and he slipped the horrible object out of her easily and then thrust his fingers into her – just as easily. It came as something of a shock to Amelia to find out how wet she was and as his fingers swirled and flexed pleasantly inside her, she did wonder if part of her hadn't wanted to see what would have happened if the infernal device had been operated.

"Come on, Robbie!" the woman called from outside and regretfully the man took his hand out of her cunt and pushed her towards the steel rail. She sat down obediently and held up her wrists to have them cuffed in steel ones whose linking chain ran round the bar. He also pulled a ball gag out of his pocket and once Amelia had opened wide he jammed it in, buckled it tight and left, slamming the door and leaving the women in pitch darkness.

Very shortly they heard the engine start and the truck lurched away. Gradually Amelia became aware that the dark was not absolute, there were small holes high up in the truck's sides. Sadia wasn't taking any chances with her livestock and Amelia was mightily relieved. She tried to get comfortable but it was impossible as the truck jerked and lurched constantly.

The journey went on and on and eventually she slipped into a restless doze but woke when her need to pee broke into her sleep. It was still dark and the truck was still on the move. She became aware of a bitter smell and realised that others had felt the same need. She looked about her and realised there was no help for it. The straw was plainly there to soak up the liquid rather than provide comfort. Slowly she clambered to her feet, and watched sympathetically by several pairs of eyes, managed to lift her skirt out of the way before she squatted down, as far away from where she was sitting as her cuffs would allow. The squalor was appalling but the relief was immense and she sank back into sleep quite quickly. But when she woke again the journey was still continuing.

Diane woke in her stall and as she did so the full realisation hit her that today she was due to be sold on.

Every muscle ached from having been run in harness and whipped almost constantly for the previous two days. But she had to put on a good show for some woman who was coming to buy her, her Mistress had told her. If she failed to sell, then her life would be a living hell, and Diane had no reason to doubt her.

The man came for her and fed her as usual, hosed her down and washed her as usual and then set about massaging her stiff muscles with all the skill he usually employed in beating her. After only a few minutes, Diane was feeling up to being harnessed again and was led outside to where a different sort of trap awaited her.

Instead of the two seater with the big wooden wheels and leather seat, a smaller one made of what looked like aluminium waited for her. As she approached it on her leash, she realised that it would be much lighter than the other one. The wheels were slightly smaller and were much thinner, with just four spokes. There was no seat, just a low platform, and the shafts were thinner too, and they joined the trap itself low down at the front and then swept up and levelled off at hand height. And where her hands would be shackled to them, the shafts sprouted upright grips that she would be able to wrap her hands around and grip tightly. The whole thing reminded her of the chariots that the Romans had raced in their arenas and circuses.

"She'll be here in an hour or so. Run it enough to get it warmed up and used to the lighter rig, then just trot it on a lunge or something till she arrives." Diane's Mistress came up from behind them and gave the man his orders. She felt the woman's hand run over her flank, the nails just digging in slightly at the welts from the whip. It was both encouragement and warning. If she didn't put on a good show, those welts would be nothing compared to what she would get.

Once she had been tacked up, she was backed between the shafts and immediately felt the difference. The man stood on the low platform, directly over the axle and only affected the balance if he moved backwards or forwards. Otherwise, it was as if he wasn't there, compared to the more stately one she was used to. She flexed her fingers around the grips and settled her grip, waiting for the inevitable lash that would signal the start of the day's work.

When it came, Diane knew that what had gone before had been a gentle introduction to the life of a pony slave. The cord was much heavier than before and thudded across her back almost as if she had been punched.

"Hiya!" the man called from behind her and before she could begin to take the strain more lashes smacked across her shoulders. She tossed her head in protest and lunged forwards desperately, finding to her amazement that she had launched straight into a full run. The chariot was so light that in comparison to the two seater, it seemed to float behind her. Still the driver wanted more speed however, and so still she was beaten mercilessly until she was stretching her legs to their maximum, her hair was flying behind her, the breeze was in her face and the plugs inside her were a torment beyond belief. Gradually the whip slowed to just a few lashes every now and then, behind her the chariot wheels rumbled softly on the grass and it jolted on the occasional rough patch, she had never run so fast. The park blurred as the cool wind made her eyes water and Diane knew that only being stopped and used by her driver could make her any more ecstatically happy. Even the bitter taste of steel from her bit seemed sweet that morning. The reins were being held much more tightly than before, making her arch her neck forwards to counter the strain and she yearned to feel the driver steer her, to emphasise her complete subjugation to him. And presently he did, bringing her steadily round to her left, flicking the whip at her left flank, making the heavy cord bite at her cunt lips. She thought it was probably to accustom her to the increased severity of the lash, rather than to correct any disobedience on her part. But now she was used to it and to the new, lighter chariot, she enjoyed the thudding impact of the whip cord.

She was finally reined in back at the front of the house where once again her Mistress kept an eye on her pulse until her breathing had calmed, she seemed well pleased and Diane was put to gentle trotting at the end of a lunge rein. Her driver stood with rein and whip in his hands and guided her in circles around him, urging her to adopt what she felt was a rather stupid prancing sort of step with her knees being lifted exaggeratedly high with each step. With her hands clipped together behind her back it took some concentration to maintain balance at times, but however silly Diane might have felt, the driver was plainly intent on her mastering the gait as he plied the whip tirelessly. So absorbed was Diane in learning this new lesson that she only heard the car crunch over the last few yards of gravel on the drive.

"Whoa!" her driver called and halted her with a lash across her stomach. Diane knew enough now to stand quite still and keep her eyes down as footsteps approached both from the house and from the direction of the car.

"Sadia! How lovely to see you again!" It was her Mistress' voice greeting someone from the car.

"Marguerite!" a female voice replied and there was the sound of an air kiss.

"And this is Eric, I don't think you've met him darling," the new voice continued. "He's my chief banker, backer, broker and general Mister Fixit."

There were introductions all round and Diane began to fidget with boredom.

"Ah! So this is the one you want me to see!" the new woman said as Diane made her bridle jingle by shaking her head irritably.

A black haired woman, tall and slender appeared at Diane's right shoulder. And once again, cool, knowledgeable hands began to explore her body. They ran across her breasts and tested the tightness of the straps that steadied them, they followed the crupper strap and pinched her labia and even her bit was taken out so that her teeth could be inspected.

"Okay, it looks well enough; good tits and not too short in the leg. You say it's one of Doc. Williams? Should be okay as far as fucking goes, she does turn out a good product for that purpose," the black haired woman said finally. "Let's see how it runs."

Her driver replaced the lunge rein with the proper steering ones and backed her up to the chariot again. As she was shackled to the two grips on the shafts, Diane was able to see the two women in whose hands her fate now lay. Her Mistress was pointing to her and remarking on something to the new woman; Diane could imagine that the conversation would be about her legs or some aspect of her body. She felt herself moisten around the dildo as she realised that she was being sold once again. She was merely a cross between a beast of burden and a whore; a pony slave, a whoreslave. The new woman was nodding her head sagely and pointing at her breasts when she felt the reins tighten as her driver mounted and braced himself, she arched her neck and then lunged forward once more as the whip clubbed at her again, reviving the fading pain from her last beating.

For the next half an hour she was run backwards and forwards in front of the new woman and the man. Each time she was turned, her driver yanked cruelly hard at the reins, making her rear and cavil at her bit as she was hauled around, then she was lashed into a full gallop until he decided to yank her round again and rain in lashes on her before she had had any chance to turn properly. It seemed to her as though he was whipping her purely for the sake of it – for the joy of it – to judge by his cries and whoops as the cord thudded across her welted skin. And the worst of it was she was helpless to do anything but adore him for it.

By the time she was drawn up again, in front of her small audience, saliva was hanging in strings from her chin and dripping coldly onto her breasts, her teeth were clenched against the unforgiving steel of the bit and her chest burned from the effort of catching her breath whilst running at full speed under the lash.

But it seemed to have done the trick, Diane realised as she panted her way back to normal breathing. Hands patted her flanks and back, voices cooed and told her she was a good pony. Gradually she began to listen more closely as she was able to calm down and stop fidgeting and stamping.

"Excellent! It's a natural for single racing and with tits like those, why not dressage as well? Have you run it with any others in a team chariot?" the new woman was enquiring eagerly.

"No, we've only had it two days. But it's got stamina and you can tell it loves the whip, so why wouldn't it run well in one of those?" her Mistress replied.

"It's the last we can buy," the man called Eric put in. "I'm afraid the cupboard's almost bare, Sadia."

"Oh, Eric!" The new woman turned on him. "You know we set out to buy the right talent when we saw it, well I've seen this one and I'm having it!"

The argument moved away and her driver smacked her bottom affectionately as he began to unshackle her wrists.

"That's a good girl. They'll buy you alright. Ran like the wind and took the whip like an old timer.... let's get you settled down and rested......after I've had some payment......well overdue I reckon!" He laughed as he finished unbridling her and clipped her hands behind her again. Then he took a fistful of hair and tugged it downwards. Diane had no option but to follow and went immediately to her knees. In front of her she could see the result of such a mad, whip-wielding gallop. The front of his trousers was bulging and Diane could almost see the thick pillar of hard flesh urgent for release.

She reflected briefly while she watched his hand unzip the flies and pull down trousers and pants, that her back and buttocks must have been wonderful targets – buttocks especially – as they shook and rippled as her feet pounded the ground and the whip ploughed bright red furrows across them.

His cock sprang free and reared imperiously in front of her face, it was immensely thick and the helm, as he drew the foreskin back, was a gloriously broad, gleaming expanse of sex flesh. She hadn't tasted cock since the border post and licked her lips now to moisten them as she leaned forwards in response to another tug on her hair and opened wide. But even at maximum stretch he seemed to touch every part of her mouth as she gently slipped her lips over him and felt the massive thing flatten her tongue as it slipped into her. He tasted delightfully clean after the border guards and Diane sucked eagerly, hollowing her cheeks. He groaned in pleasure above her and dug his other hand into her hair and began to urge her backwards and forwards. Her time with Madam had shown Diane how much she enjoyed being used by a man in this way and she made no move to resist him using her head to mouth fuck her. She knew with complete, calm, certainty that she couldn't wait for him to come, to feel his cock swell and leap and spurt the powerful tasting liquor, she rather hoped he would make her choke on the power and quantity of his climax. She always got a jolt of excitement deep in her belly when a man overcame her so completely just by the power of his ejaculation.

Slowly her driver increased the speed of the thrusts he was making her head take, Diane felt him drive deeper into her throat with each one and tried to relax as she had been taught. She rather wished that the whip that had taught her could be there now as he really did thrust for her depths. His pubic hair rasped and tickled her nose for a second before she was drawn back and on the next stroke she felt him pause and within her stuffed mouth, the shaft of his cock began to swell and pump and Diane readied herself for the onslaught as his hands held her head tightly down onto him.

Suddenly his hips began to jerk and his cock was pushed even further down her throat, just as she felt the divine power of the surges within the hard shaft as the sperm was pumped up to be ejaculated into her. Trying to hang onto the calm that Madam had beaten into her, Diane opened her throat and welcomed the bitter harvest, spurt after spurt. And she almost made it, but just when she would have expected most cocks to have finished, this one didn't and yet more spunk was splashed into her throat and she could no longer keep herself open. Helplessly she began to choke and then panic as the stuff kept coming and flooded up her nose and squeezed out around the shaft to seep onto her chin, until finally he pushed her head away from him and stood over her, smiling.

"Not bad at all!" he told her, bending down to grip her hair again and pulling her upright, still retching and coughing. "They don't usually take that much down!"

It was only as her throat and her vision cleared that she realised that a truck had pulled up alongside them while she had been used and the driver was grinning down at her.

"I can recommend the fellation at this establishment," her driver called up casually, as he dragged her towards her stable.

"May well try it once I get these bitches in the back bedded down!" the truck driver called back.

"Just let me get this one hobbled and I'll help you," Diane's driver replied and pushed her roughly into her stable, chained her by one ankle to the wall and left her.

CHAPTER 10

Negotiations had carried on for most of the evening but finally a price had been agreed for Diane and in the office, in Marguerite's house, Eric put the phone down and glowered at Sadia. "There, the money's transferred and that's it, Sadia. We have a full complement and you must make it work with what we have."

"Alright, Eric! Do stop banging on about money! I know we've got a full stable now and, yes, I'll make it a success. Now just calm down and choose a slave from this last lot to enjoy in Marguerite's special room. I think a celebration's in order!"

Eric's face cleared suddenly as he savoured the prospect of enjoying part of the new stable's livestock.

"How about that one we picked up back in Kiev, the one with the nicely upturned nipples. Let's have her."

Sadia put an arm round his shoulders and chuckled. "That's better! You're looking happier already."

Amelia was woken by the light in the dormitory being turned on suddenly and one of the men from the truck walking forward to unchain her wrists from the bars of the bedhead.

In groups of three the girls had been unloaded from the truck, allowed to wash, been given food and then been put to bed on simple army beds, their wrist cuffs imprisoning them before a single blanket was pulled over them. When they had all been processed the light was turned out and the door was locked. They were housed in what seemed to be part of a stableyard and some light found its way in through small windows set high up in the walls. They let in some sound as well.

Faintly they could hear male voices and laughter and then the sound of doors opening and closing. The voices went quiet for a while and then there was the unmistakable heavy smacking of a flogger being plied. Amelia's imagination supplied the image of a lucky girl twisting and writhing under the flogging before being fucked. Around her was silence, even though the girls could have talked, and she guessed that the others were thinking roughly the same thoughts. There were even some furtive rustlings as legs were parted and then thighs clenched in frustration; and Amelia smiled as she realised hers were too. Whoever this Sadia woman was, she had clearly invested in some well trained girlflesh she thought as she struggled to block out the seductive noises and get some sleep. It would not be long before she had to perform for her new owner after all.

Sleep had come surprisingly quickly and the next thing she knew was the man hauling her out of bed and clipping her wrists behind her again. Then with no word of explanation he bent, grabbed her legs and hoisted her over his shoulder. Then he set off towards the house and Amelia came fully awake as the biting cold of the air cleared her head.

He took her into a warm kitchen and set her down. She looked around and saw two other men one of whom was holding a leather hood and he smiled as he approached her.

"They want you," was all he said before the scented darkness of leather descended over her.

Eric slowly ran his loosely clenched fist up and down the hard shaft of his cock as he stood naked in Marguerite's special room. In amongst the array of winches and frames and racks of whips, canes and crops and dildos and plugs, was a huge bed with four wrought iron posts, supporting a canopy. All four posts were equipped with suspension rings and iron dildos jutting upwards from them. On the scarlet sheets, Sadia and Marguerite had already got the party underway. Their two, tanned and slender bodies entwined, both quite naked. At the moment they lay face to face, kissing each other deeply and passionately, he knew they were old friends and colleagues in the slave running business – and that was why he had stuck out for a lower price on the final slave. Sadia would have agreed to anything just to get Marguerite into bed. To some extent he could sympathise, the woman was magnificent – almost as superb as Sadia herself. As he watched them, the bulges of their breasts as they pressed against one another beckoned to his fingers. Their long thighs rubbing and their thick, dark hair entangling, their smooth buttocks, all seemed to him to beg for cock and whip……..But he knew that it was not really so.

Occasionally Sadia would allow him to fuck her and vouchsafe visions of paradise as her strong body took him for rides so exhilarating that no other woman had ever run her close. But even then, when he had finished ejaculating into her, there would be a slavegirl standing by to lick her clean of his emissions.

It was only with another woman that she truly gave herself.

On the bed the two took a break from kissing, sipped at their glasses of wine on the bedside tables and Sadia swivelled around to face down Marguerite's body. With earthy chuckles that nearly had Eric coming over his hand, the two came together again, this time in a sixty-nine. The forthcoming session with the slave would be mainly for his release while his lady, his icon of unapproachable feminine beauty, disported herself with her friend.

The slave would take all his frustrations – and he couldn't wait to start releasing them. He watched Sadia's head bobbing up and down between Marguerite's widespread thighs.

The door opened briefly and the slave was pushed in. She stumbled uncertainly to a stop as soon as she could, because her head was tightly buckled into a thick leather hood that encased her from her nose upwards. The eyes and ears were covered in reinforced pads, leaving her only her mouth and nostrils. Her wrists were clipped tidily together behind her back and she wore four inch heeled, black court shoes. The black of the leather at her wrists and ankles, shoes and hood contrasted delightfully with the pallor of her skin. Her breasts with their tip-tilted nipples – already hard and erect, he noted – were heaving prettily as she breathed nervously. He could almost see her quivering with terrified anticipation. Of course she would know she was going to be used but – and he cast a glance at the bed where both women were taking a break from cunnilingus and were looking up at the silent figure of the slave – she could have no idea about who was going to use her. Or how hard her use would be. Sadia was in celebratory mood and he was jealous. It could be a long night for this slave.

Amelia could hear her heart thundering as she stood, braced and uncertain, with no idea of where she was or who – if anyone – was with her. Suddenly she jumped and cried out. A hand had touched her; touched her breast. Her face was slapped hard and she thought she caught the sound of an angry voice. Then the hand was back and this time she felt the fingers tighten around her right nipple and pull then twist it. Immediately she felt better as the pain speared through her, overcoming her fear by stoking the lust that being used always provoked in her. It had been so long! Danny had done his best, but not since her last visit to The Lodge and the flogging at the holding camp had someone really tested her. Now another hand was at her left nipple and she braced herself against the pull on the hard little nuggets, but a push at her back made her stumble forwards and the hands left her nipples but held her arms, then guided her downwards. She knelt, but that wasn't enough, again a shove in her back and another on the back of her head made her kneel back on her heels and then slip forwards onto the floor face down. She felt a heeled shoe press against the back of her neck at the same time as she felt heavy karabiners being clipped to her ankle cuffs. Her heart leaped, at last she was being used properly – anonymously, brutally. Just as an arena slave ought to be.

Her ankles came under tension, then more tension and as she bit her lip to stop herself from crying out, she felt her legs being inexorably drawn up behind her. The strain on her hips was terrible as her torso left the ground and then she was swinging wildly in the air; terrified of hitting something. But there was no impact and slowly her body settled to hanging still. Her legs and hips feeling wrenched.

Hands began to rove over her again. Now they explored her back and buttocks and at last ran along the length of her slit, exposed between her wide spread thighs, stroking the soft lips that parted eagerly to reveal the juicy interior. Amelia knew she was inviting every sort of mistreatment a dominant could devise but also knew she was helpless to do anything else. Had been even before she had been abducted and trained.

But even so she jumped in her bonds when a long length of something soft caressed her groin and inner thighs. It was laid down so that it trailed along her vulva and down the crack of her bottom onto her back and was then slowly drawn back so that she had plenty of time to make the acquaintance of the whip that was about to beat her.

Amelia relaxed and prepared for the ride ahead. She was in the hands of people who knew how to treat girls like her.

When the first lash arrived, a firework display went off in the darkness of the hood and her thighs stung immediately. After three more, she knew she was in for a long night. Whoever was beating her was throwing themselves into their work. Amelia wished with all her heart that she could see herself hanging upside down, legs spread to expose her cunt, twisting and crying out under the lash in preparation for whatever her masters or mistresses wanted to do to her.

The next morning she eased herself against the cold steel of the truck's body. Even through the rough weave of the short coats they had been issued with, she was tender.

She had awoken back in her bed and had been the recipient of admiring stares from the others as they were allowed to wash and breakfast before being loaded back into the truck. One more girl – a tousle haired, big busted brunette she hadn't seen before - had been shoved in and chained, then the doors had been slammed and the truck had moved off. Now the diesel growled and clattered and the truck bumped and lurched over potholes and subsidence. The coats they had been given had three buttons down the front and only covered them to mid-thigh, though they were welcome nonetheless as the air was still cold, and Amelia cast a professional eye over the long, shapely, athletic legs on display. After her experiences the night before and now, looking around her sister-slaves, she was quite certain she had fallen exactly where she wanted to be – into the hands of someone who really knew the arenas. She just wasn't certain yet who her owner was. Was it the woman who had claimed her after the auction? Or was she merely an agent? But there again, hadn't Carlo and Brian mentioned something about a female owner a few months back? Whatever......she had been treated mercilessly the night before and with a sigh of pleasure she settled back, deliberately making her welted back and bottom sting all over again.

The crotch whipping had been long and expert; slow and cruel. She had never been given a chance to get into any rhythm. The lashes had fallen at irregular intervals, and then another lash had started falling across her bottom. So there were at least two dominants working on her. They had made her twist and at last cry out when the pain grew too great. It was early in the session and she knew she could take a lot more yet but it would need other treatments before the pleasure overcame the pain.

They knew that.

They hauled her up a little further and then she cried out again and jumped in shock as something touched her stinging cunt. It was the broad curve of a dildo head pushing down into her seething, molten and burning cunt. It slid on and on, filling her, making her moan with pleasure. And then it was turned on. She opened her mouth wide to yell in delight and found a flesh and blood cock waiting for her. The cry faded into an undignified gurgle as the cock pushed in and she thought she caught the faint sound of female laughter.

But that was irrelevant as her world now consisted of the insistent vibration in her cunt that was driving her mad as she couldn't close her thighs or use her hands, and the hard, hot shaft of cock that was going to ejaculate into her upside down mouth at any moment. She braced herself to swallow and nearly drowned in pride as she managed to force every spurt up her throat. Once the cock had finished with her, someone pumped the dildo until she came.

They took her down after that and she discovered a third dominant. She was pushed onto what she assumed was a bed and her face was forced against a wet vulva, smelling pungently of a recent orgasm. Amelia hoped her beating might have inspired that and she stuck out her tongue and got to work. Again, it had been so long since she had tasted a woman. Not since she had sneaked a quickie with Purdy in her stall at The Lodge on the last morning of her final visit had she felt and tasted the thick outpourings of cunt sap. She guzzled it down greedily and then dissolved into helpless moans of delight as she felt cold lubricant being spread round her anus. The only way she was able to discern that what entered her was a strap-on was the smoothness of the thighs against her own as the shaft was slid remorselessly into her narrowest passage.

And as she tongued the cunt in front of her and was shafted from behind, a heavy strap was plied across her shoulders. Whoever was wielding it moved from one side of the bed to the other and wrapped her with it so that the sides of her breasts and her upper arms were scored as well. As the flogging progressed, the cunt she was licking remained still, so somehow the flagellator was managing to miss the spread thighs she was lying between. Skilful.

Eventually she felt the woman in front of her shudder into orgasm, closely followed by the one buggering her and at last she herself came. Respite was short lived, however.

They turned her onto her back, bound her breasts, whipped them and then hot waxed them. Each drop of wax exploding into her darkness and burning just a little brighter before fading. Amelia was lost, she could hold onto rational thought no more and allowed herself to be driven wherever they wanted her. She climaxed again and again, she licked cunt till her tongue ached and her face ran with juice. She was fucked by the man at one point, but in between which torments she couldn't recall.

She was stood up and suspended by her wrists, beaten to orgasm again and then fucked with a strap-on from in front, a woman's breasts rubbing sweetly, amidst all the raging pains, against her own swollen and still-bound ones.

As far as she could remember, after that she had been laid back on the bed, tied in an X shape on her back and what felt like fire had been fed into her almost steaming cunt. She had yelled in unashamed terror until a liquid slushing had betrayed the presence of ice cubes.

Amelia shifted uncomfortably on her straw as the truck lurched around a corner. Her memories were making her sting and burn all over again and she could feel that she was leaking moisture. A woman's buttocks had been pressed over her face soon after that and as she probed between them with her tongue, she had met another tongue, working at the front door. She had come when a man's weight had been added and his cock had slid into the swamp of her cunt and ridden her to multiple orgasms the like of which she had scarcely ever achieved – even in her early days with Brian.......

"Anyone know what's going to happen to us?"

A tremulous voice broke into her thoughts and Amelia opened her eyes. The brunette who had only joined them that morning had spoken and was looking around, terrified of her own audacity in speaking.

But it seemed she had broken the spell and as no immediate male retribution was forthcoming, suddenly the girls began to look at each other and stir.

"Judging by the exercise routine, I'd say we're for the arenas." It was an American voice and Amelia looked opposite her to the blonde who had spoken.

"Yes," Amelia confirmed. "I'd agree."

"The arenas?" the brunette practically squeaked. "Oh my God! I mean I've heard bits......they do terrible things to girls there!"

Amelia looked at the brunette with a wry grin. Where had the girl been? The arenas were so much an accepted part of internet life for those who couldn't afford to attend in person that they were almost mainstream – despite being illegal and being constantly condemned by politicians who unaccountably failed to legislate against them. In spite of the urgings of some female MPs. Most of the arenas now had at least one, large smoked glass box and it was widely suspected that public figures, who could not afford to be seen at an event, paid astronomical sums to watch in safety.

"Seems like they got started in right away on you honey," the American blonde said, addressing the brunette.

The girl looked down at her thighs, with their still livid tracery of driving whip welts – Amelia knew them so well.

"Yes, all three of them last night, and that was after a day of running as a pony......" the girl looked down and Amelia was amused to see a flash of pride in her eyes. She was a true slave. And she had already been put between the shafts of a chariot or a trap. That was one up on Amelia and the rest as it turned out.

The brunette shrugged modestly. "I don't know why, they just seemed to think I'd be good." She looked around, blushing. "My name's Diane by the way."

Hesitantly they all gave their names. There were two Americans as it turned out, Jan and Kirsty, there were also several East Europeans and one heavily built girl from Siberia – who could speak no English but could communicate through a Bulgarian student of languages. There was a Finnish girl and several more Middle Eastern girls.

"It's nice to meet you all," the blonde American said when they had all introduced themselves. "But where we're going, we won't need names, we'll just be numbers."

"And we probably won't be able to talk anyway," Amelia told them.

Several of the girls looked at her with horrified puzzlement on their faces.

"Most stables tongue ring their slaves now," Amelia went on. "My boyfriend was a fan," she added hastily.

"She's right," someone chimed in. "No one want to know what you say. Just want to see you fight and run."

"And fuck," the other American put in.

There were rueful smiles as the realisation that they all knew what they had become, crept over them.

"And take the whip," Diane said, stretching out a long thigh and turning it this way and that to examine her welts.

Amelia did the same and smiled at her. "Oh yes! Cock and the whip."

"The bastards've got us nailed!" the blonde American said chuckling.

There was general, rueful laughter as the truck carried the final recruits to their destination.

CHAPTER 11

They made an overnight stop and the girls slept on the hard floor of the truck, once it had been hosed out. The three men who guarded them cooked over an open fire and if any of the girls had entertained thoughts of escape with so small an escort, one of the men had banished them as soon as they had stumbled down, stiff and sore onto the grass on which the truck had been parked.

"Take a good look around, ladies," he invited them.

Amelia did and realised that they had descended from the mountains and were now on the edge of a tundra. The air was still cold and scrub grassland seemed to stretch away into infinity in front of them. If she turned slightly to look behind her, the mountains still loomed in the distance. They turned round and round, looking from horizon to horizon, there was no sign of any human habitation. The space seemed so great that Amelia almost felt a strange sort of panic and a dizziness, she glanced along the line of slaves and realised that she was not alone, pale faces stared at the desolation in horror.

The man who had spoken smiled. "Makes us seem kinda homely, doesn't it? There are packs of hunting dogs out there too. So really, really don't try anything stupid."

In small groups they were led to a stream and allowed to wash and go behind some low bushes to perform what they had managed to refrain from doing in the truck.

The supper was good; baked potatoes and thick, smoked sausage. Again they ate in small groups so only a few of them ever had the use of their hands at any one time and then they were herded back into the truck to sleep. Amelia found herself next to the other

English girl who had introduced herself as Diane. They were given slightly longer chains on their wrists so that they could at least lie down. And as they lay, they listened to the slaves the three men had chosen put to use up against the sides of the truck.

It was typically quick and casual, the truck body rocked slightly on its suspension as the girls were lifted up against the sides and fucked, their short coats just lifted enough to give access to what the men wanted. Amelia caught Diane's eye as they sat and swayed with the movement as the girls moaned and the men grunted until they achieved their release. They both realised that their expressions were ones of pure envy.

The three girls were duly returned with snail trails of sperm on their thighs. One of the Americans, the blonde, had been used, the Siberian girl who smiled shyly as she settled down and looked proudly at the traces of her usage, and one of the Middle Eastern ones. The American blonde summed up the girls' feelings with a whispered comment as the doors slammed shut for the night.

"Can't be all bad if there's more who can fuck like that guy!"

The night was bitterly cold and the girls huddled together for warmth. Amelia and Diane found that they had sufficient slack in their chains to be able to clasp each other round the neck and so were able to hollow out a small space in the straw bedding and sleep with their legs entwined and their bodies clasped together. During the night Amelia woke several times to hear soft rustlings and mews of pleasure as pairs of girls succumbed to the temptation offered by a warm thigh pressed between their own. Eventually she joined in and rubbed Diane to an orgasm before the brunette returned the favour and they sank back into deep sleep.

Three of the girls were lucky enough to get a hot breakfast, courtesy of the men's cocks the next morning and Amelia was among them. Otherwise they had to make do with a drink of ice cold water from the stream and then they were on their way again.

Not until the evening did they finally reach journey's end. The truck stopped and they heard the men calling out and other men's voices replying, then there was the squeal of metal on metal as gates swung open and the truck entered somewhere, stopped at last and the doors were flung back.

The first person to enter was a woman.

She wore a pair of jodhpurs; brown, knee high boots and a crisp white blouse under a short jacket. Her hair was blonde and thick and it hung over her shoulders in glossy, well kept waves. She swept it back with one hand as her nose wrinkled at the acrid smell of the truck.

"Tell Sadia that the last lot is here!" she called to someone outside and then swaggered the length of the truck, surveying its cargo.

"Personally I think you're a waste of her money," she sneered in clipped, precise, home counties English. "But we'll make something less ghastly out of you in due course."

Standing neat, pressed and groomed above the dishevelled slaves, she woke instant fury in Amelia. It was one thing to be dominated and abused by men, but this sneering bitch would have earned herself a sound thrashing from Carlo for such arrogance – guaranteed to raise the hackles on even the most docile slave and disturb the good order of a stable.

She was about to make a vocal protest when the American blonde beat her to it.

"Sister, just 'cos you got a rod up your ass, don't take it out on us!"

A nasty smile spread across the woman's face as she went to stand over the American.

"Thank you, you dumb cow. There's always one that'll rise to the bait."

She strode to the back of the truck and jumped down with athletic ease and they could hear her giving instructions as she marched away. The slaves' eyes followed her and took in the scene.

The truck was parked in a sort of stockade surrounded by high walls of stone. Within the walls were several long, low buildings with small windows, again they were built of stone and looked as though they had been built to withstand some harsh conditions. The centre of the stockade was simply bare earth and was an area the size of several football pitches. On the far side of it, and partly built into the perimeter wall, was a large house. Amelia took it all in and especially noted the tall wooden stakes driven into the ground in the centre area. She knew a gladiatorial training area when she saw one and also knew whipping posts when she saw them. Squinting her eyes against the setting sun, she could also make out, beyond the big house, the roof line of an arena.

She had made it at long last.

It took all her self control not to leap with joy as her feet touched the earth when they were all released and helped down to stand in a huddled group at the back of the truck, awaiting developments.

There didn't seem to be anyone around apart from the three men who had brought them and a few more who had appeared and were now smoking and chatting around the truck.

"I don't think that bitch has just gone for a coffee break," the American whispered to Diane, who was standing beside Amelia.

As if to prove the truth of that statement, things started to happen quite quickly.

Doors in several of the low stone buildings swung open and crowds of naked women began to emerge, driven by men and women with whips which they cracked over their charges' heads. From the house came a group of people, among whom Diane recognised the figure of the woman who she thought had bought her from her Mistress. Slowly the naked women were herded into a crowd around a cleared area occupied by the party from the house. As the crowd formed, the men began to chivvy Diane's and Amelia's little party towards the main group.

As they approached, Amelia could feel the suppressed excitement in the air, the toned, naked arena slaves who wore their nudity with casual self assurance were smiling and several had their arms draped over the shoulders of the girl next to them. Amelia was surprised at the openly expressed affection she saw as they came closer, there were even some kisses and some stroking of breasts. This was not how any stable she had ever seen before had functioned.

The men cleared a path for their party through the naked throng by smacking any flesh that came their way and a path opened up that led them through to the centre.

Standing with the sneering blonde woman was a tall dark haired one who spoke directly to them once they had reached the front of the crowd.

"I am the Countess Sadia de Groncourt and I own you and this whole stable," she said succinctly. And then she gestured to the woman beside her. "And this is Angelica Smythe. She is my chief trainer."

"Oh shit," whispered the American beside her.

Angelica stepped forwards and calmly shrugged off her jacket then began to unbutton her blouse. She nodded at the blonde American.

"That's the one I'll take down, my lady."

"You, step out here!" the woman called Sadia called. "You insulted my chief trainer! You will pay a heavy price for that stupidity and all your friends will see what happens to you!"

Two men grabbed the American and ripped her coat from her then thrust her into the ring formed by the crowd.

Angelica shrugged off her blouse and reached behind her to unclip her bra, a sigh went up from the assembled slaves as her magnificent breasts swung free and pale, their tips crowned with deep red nipples, standing out hard and erect with excitement.

"I'm going to teach you respect, you mouthy little slut!" Angelica spat and began to unbutton her jodhpurs while circling the perimeter of the makeshift ring.

The American knew that whether or not she wanted one, a fight was inevitable and while the trainer's hands were busy she rushed in.

An elegantly booted foot lifted effortlessly to chest height and stopped her dead, dumping her, winded, on the earth.

And while the slave writhed and gasped on the ground, the trainer calmly divested herself of the rest of her clothes until she was wearing only a brief, lacy thong.

Amelia could feel the lust coming off the slaves as they drank in the sight of their trainer stripped for action but strangely the men seemed quite unmoved.

Angelica was a superb specimen, she exuded strength without exhibiting anything as vulgar or unfeminine as overly developed muscle, she was trim, smooth, heavily breasted, long legged and drop-dead gorgeous. Only Blondie herself looked better naked, Amelia thought as the woman ghosted in towards the American, who was clumsily regaining her feet.

It wasn't a fight at all. It was clinical destruction and Amelia realised as she watched it amidst growing cheers from the other slaves, it must be a deliberate ploy each time a new batch of slaves arrived. Angelica would trap one of them into talking back and use her to demonstrate to the others what she was capable of.

She unleashed four or five straight jabs to the American's body before she could react, then slipped down and tripped her with a leg scissors, making fall onto her face, before she climbed onto her back, twisting one arm and then grabbing a breast. Slowly she increased the grip she had on the unfortunate slave's tit and the crowd all watched her expression change as the pain registered until she was screaming and wriggling ineffectually under the trainer. Then Angelica let her go and stood back.

The American came up almost demented with fury and charged again. This time she was thrown bodily into the crowd, carving a swathe in the naked ranks, there was good natured laughter and she was thrown back in before she knew what was happening. She staggered drunkenly into the centre of the ring and Angelica grabbed an arm, swung her round and simply released her to collide face first with the crowd – one of whom, Amelia clearly saw, put a forearm up to stop her. The American went down like a stone and Angelica had to help her up before she could hoist the inert girl onto her shoulders, spin round and then, when she was completely dizzy, drop her onto the earth and sink down to kneel triumphantly on her fallen foe.

The cheering was deafening as the slaves acknowledged the downfall of a fellow slave and as Angelica knelt over the American's face and twisted her nipples savagely to make her buck and writhe under her, Amelia had to admire the psychology that had gone into it. Reinforce the trainer's dominance by humiliating another slave and let the new slaves know they were the lowest of the low.

Sadia walked forwards and held up a hand for silence, which she got instantly.

"Put the creature in solitary. The rest return to barracks. Have the new ones wait here."

Two men appeared as Angelica stood up and grabbed the American, dragging her behind them as they took her to one side of the central area.

"Watch this, all of you," Sadia told the huddled party of newcomers. "These are the solitary cells. You really won't like them so don't get sent there!"

As they watched, to their horror they saw one of the men pick up a heavy rope and pull on it. It dragged up from ground level a large iron grating that had been set into the earth.

Then they simply pushed the American girl into the pit it had covered, she disappeared with a despairing scream and a thump.

"She'll keep for a week or so and will be amenable to discipline afterwards. Regrettably in a big organisation like this," Angelica told them as she zipped up her boots with hardly a hair on her head out of place. "People don't always have time to observe the usual customs of life....."

As they continued to watch, one of the men unzipped his flies and urinated into the pit. Amelia looked at

Angelica with astonishment, this was much harsher discipline than she had ever come across.

The trainer treated them all to a slow smile. "And you'd be amazed by the number of slaves who get caught short when there's someone in solitary. Everyone needs to have someone to look down on!"

And with that she sauntered away back to the house.

"Now listen to me!" Sadia told them sternly. "You've seen the tip of the iceberg, that's all! She'll be taken out several times, whipped and put back. She'll be begging to be allowed to lick Angelica's boots by the end."

She strode up and down the line with two male guards and two women who were dressed as Angelica had been, standing facing the row of cowed slaves — among whose number Amelia now found herself.

She had never expected anything like this.

"Let me explain," Sadia went on. "We're the only female owned stable on the circuit. We've got the only female trainer. We're the Girl Squad and the guys who train the other stables can't wait to thrash us. They reckon we'll turn out some girlie girls who'll roll over and eat pussy as soon as they get hit with a whip for the first time. I've had to have my best fighters win five bouts in a row with studded whips just to get a first event. My racing chariots have had to win three races in the same morning at private venues to get taken seriously.

"And now that I've got you lot, the last I needed to bring me up to a full complement of a hundred squad fighters with ten solo fighters, we've got a first date for a full three day event. It's in Bakhtar and it's in eight weeks." She stopped for a moment and looked at them. "Even then the Owners' Council won't sanction a full arena event in case we don't give value for money, but if we can win – we're in! And we will! Every girl in my stable will be whipped day in and day out until she takes it like breathing. They'll be the hardest, best, fittest and meanest on the circuit!"

The last words were spoken with such passion that Amelia found herself almost cheering the woman on, despite the fact that it was she, as a slave, who would bear the brunt of the savage training regime.

"I'm going to be hard on you! And Angelica doesn't know any other way, thanks to the English public school system. But you'll need to stand together when you're out there taking on the enemy. They'll have been driven just as hard because no one wants to lose to the Girl Squad! So you'll learn to stand together like no other squad, so discipline within the barracks is relaxed and if you haven't had sex with a girl before, get used to it now! Tongue ringing and chipping tomorrow. Training starts the day after. Take them away!" She turned on her heel and marched away while the guards herded them towards one end of one of the low buildings Amelia had noted when they first arrived.

Her thoughts raced as they were marched towards what had to be their barracks. The American girl's humiliation and punishment had shocked her and she was struggling to understand what Sadia had told them – at least she understood why they were going to have be twice as good as the opposition to be taken seriously, it was just her later remarks about sex with other girls. Slaves had sex wherever they could and with whoever wanted them. Didn't they?

A female guard produced a bunch of keys and unlocked a heavy wooden door.

"Welcome to you new home, ladies!" she said with a mocking bow and a smile. Deeply distrusting, the new batch stepped into the twilight of the room beyond.

For a while they stood motionless after the door had slammed shut while their eyes accustomed to the gloom. Slowly the room was revealed. A row of simple iron framed beds stood against the far wall. Over to their left was a table with two long bench seats on either side and an open plan shower and toilet room was beyond that.

In front of them stood about twenty of the stable's established contingent of slaves.

One of them stepped forwards and smiled broadly, not as a gesture of friendship but to display the heaviest tongue ring Amelia had ever seen. The girl's gaze swept past Amelia and came to light on Diane. Immediately she made for her but one of the others stepped forwards and

tripped her up, grabbing Diane for herself. The first girl punched up from the floor and caught the second girl a thudding blow right between the legs. She went down instantly and Amelia didn't see what happened next because someone grabbed her, spun her round and was kissing her before she knew what was happening. The steel of the tongue ring clanked and battered at her teeth as she fought to free herself, and suddenly she was free. But only because the girl who had grabbed her initially had herself been grabbed and claimed and was on her knees, passionately licking at another girl's crotch. The standing girl looked over at Amelia and snarled threateningly.

Someone else spun Amelia round and this time a hand found its way into her coat and gripped her breast. A tongue ring slithered up and down her neck and Amelia felt another hand groping at her crotch. It was clear that within the barracks, it was a free for all and what was happening now was old hands staking a claim on new meat. She saw Diane give in to the inevitable and start taking her coat off as a tall black haired girl fought off the groping hands of two smaller slaves. She looked over to the beds and saw the Siberian girl already with her legs spread and a slave's head bobbing eagerly at her cunt while another knelt over her face. Almost without realising it she started undoing her coat as she struggled to define what it was that was wrong with the beds.

There weren't enough. That was what had been bothering her ever since they came in, she realised. The hands belonged to a Nordic blonde type who smiled at Amelia as her coat fell open and she bent her head to suckle at her nipples. Before she gave herself over to pleasure, Amelia realised that no one ever slept alone in these barracks, they would all have lovers, favourites, casual screws, but they would all know each other intensely well by the time they entered the arena. You didn't need speech to know that you fancied this or that girl, or loved the way this or that one licked you out. And if you wanted her that night, then you would make sure your owner was pleased with you or you might end up in the solitary confinement pits.

While her thoughts raced, she allowed herself to be led towards a bed and lay down on it while another fight over her took place and a Chinese looking girl emerged triumphant, ignoring a bleeding lip and scratched breasts. She smiled at Amelia and reached under the bed to produce a huge strap-on. Diane looked at the girth of the thing with trepidation. It5 was made of black plastic and made no attempt to resemble the male member, it was simply a huge rod, made to test and stimulate a vagina to its limits. Of course an arena slave had to serve in bed as well as anywhere else and a good seeing to with something that size would make sure she didn't get out of practice just because she was having lesbian sex for most of the time.

She backed up the bed, not at all sure that even with all her experience she could handle the thickness of that monster.

The Chinese girl didn't seem to be bothered and just kept smiling and advancing, buckling the thing on around her waist and between her legs. Eventually making a lunge for her and trapping her under her body. Amelia could feel the slimy thing between her legs and hoped it was lube she was feeling. All around her she could hear the moans and cries of the other new slaves as they were tried out, fought over, kept or discarded. The Chinese girl on top of Amelia, reached down between them and took hold of the strap-on, aimed it and then thrust with her pelvis. It lodged at Amelia's entrance and with her smile never flickering once the girl slammed her hips time and again into Amelia, making no attempt at foreplay, just aiming to ravish her with the monster. Eventually it was the surrounding orgy that did the trick. On the bed beside her, Diane, kneeling and with her backside in the air was being buggered and was climaxing noisily. A Greek looking blonde was kneeling behind her with glazed eyes as she reamed her backside and the clit rasper for a second made her the equal of any woman of rank or wealth, in the parity of orgasm.

Amelia let out a guttural moan as the huge thing finally slid into her and filled every centimetre of her vagina and stimulated it until she quivered in delight. She reached up and embraced the Chinese girl, bringing her face down to hers and accepting the heavy tongue ring into her own mouth in a symbolic gesture of submission as the new kid on the block. She gasped into her new lover's mouth with every lunge that filled her to the neck of her womb. And a few minutes later they both joined their voices to the chorus that surrounded them.

But of course that was not the end of things. Although the alpha members of the squad had slaked their thirsts first, there were plenty of others who wanted their turn with the fresh meat.

It was only the arrival of the evening meal that brought their use to an end. And by that time, Amelia was a wreck. The session at the house had drained her in any case and by the time a steaming urn was delivered to the barracks and everyone went to eat, she felt as though she was on fire in both her vagina and her rectum. Her anus was beyond painful, her breasts were scratched raw and her tongue ached from licking cunt.

Diane took pity on her and, rousing herself from the next bed, she helped Amelia across to the table where they found bowls, helped themselves to a rich and tasty stew and squeezed onto the benches. The other slaves ate hurriedly and Amelia could see some of the lower status ones trying to make up to the higher status ones by offering them titbits from their own food. Some were obviously devoted couples and played with each other even as they ate. The heavy tongue rings coupled with the relative freedom, resulted in a strangely animal scene where growls and snarls were used if gestures didn't suffice. Fights were almost constant as normal female bitchiness was not an option – Amelia realised.

They could shower and wash as much as they liked but again, rank was clearly delineated and some slaves served other slaves, kneeling and washing them, helping them dry their hair and brush it. Diane and Amelia began to keep together, not daring to speak –

Amelia had a feeling, one that Diane obviously shared – that if they took advantage of that freedom allowed them just this one night, the others might not like it. Instinctively they found themselves adopting a loving couple type of role to try and deter too much attention, but even so, Diane was dragged off to bed by a tall black girl and Amelia found herself claimed by a brunette with tattoos on her back and breasts when the lights went out. During the night the continual shoving and barging for possession went on. Amelia woke up at some stage to find a different girl rolling the tattooed one out of bed. There was a short fight, that had two naked bodies rolling and struggling on top of her in the dark before the new girl banished the original one and climbed in beside Amelia, grabbing her hair and forcing her face down into the hot moistness of her crotch. Amelia groaned inwardly but set about yet another session of cunt licking with as much enthusiasm as she could muster.

CHAPTER 12

The first two weeks were an unending education for Amelia and Diane's batch; and there were changes for the main body of the squad too. The very next morning, the entire squad was herded out of their various barracks and bullied and lashed into a long, sullen, bored queue. As each girl filed past a desk at the head of the queue a stencil was held against her stomach and then her lower back and a number was spray painted onto her. Amelia's number was ninety-seven.

Sadia and Angelica stood and watched the process, slapping riding crops against their thighs and taking what Amelia felt was a prurient interest in the naked women being paraded before them. Sadia referred to the Englishwoman as 'Angel', an irony that Amelia found hard to stomach when the drenched and shivering American was hauled up out of her pit, hosed down and then given thirty lashes in front of the whole squad.

Angelica carried out the sentence with a wicked looking length of supple hide, whose tail was barely an inch wide.

The bedraggled blonde had been tied to a post only by her wrists and was able to twist and flinch and try to evade the lash to her heart's content. She failed miserably to dodge a single one, 'Angel' was as gifted a flagellator as Amelia had ever seen. But the desperate attempts by the victim provided excellent entertainment for the squad who laughed and jeered at her antics while cheering their trainer on. Amelia felt it was safest to do so as well.

However, they had more things to worry about during that first week. The newcomers had to be chipped and ringed.

Amelia was well-acquainted with this procedure of course and it had been the part of her voluntary enslavement that had given her most trouble. She appreciated that an arena slave had no use for speech and that a tongue ring helped with her complete submission to her stable as well as rendering her more able to give good oral service. But inwardly she dreaded not being given a local anaesthetic; Carlo always used one because it saved time and trouble, he said. However he always branded without one because he said it helped the slave bond with her stable. At least at Sadia's stable she hadn't seen any brands, but she could not be sure that other stables would feel the same as Carlo when it came to ringing. So by the time she was chipped she could feel her knees trembling. The procedure was carried out by a woman in a white coat in a tiled room on the ground floor of the house they had seen the previous day. To judge by the array of stretcher-like benches, adjustable, dentist-type chairs and rows of bottles and syringes, this was the stable's sickbay. The woman sat behind a steel desk and beckoned Amelia across when she was ushered in by one of the female guards, who took the opportunity to feel her bottom as she passed and then followed on behind, making Amelia more conscious of her nudity than she had been for weeks.

The woman seemed to ignore her for a second as she typed information into her computer, then nodded at the guard who shoved her towards a T shaped whipping post that seemed very out of place among the medical equipment.

Nevertheless, Amelia's arms were spread out along the cross piece of the T and her wrists shackled, then her hair was piled forwards to bare her neck. She had done the same for all the CSL slaves and was pretty certain the process was painless.

The doctor came to stand in front of her and looked her in the eye.

"You no longer have a name, of course. You are simply number ninety-seven of the de Groncourt stable, fighting in my lady's colours of yellow and black. As you gain experience so this chip will contain more information so that if you should be sold on, a buyer will know what he's getting. When the chip is implanted you will be tongue ringed so this is probably the last time anyone will address you as a person at all, ninety-seven."

Amelia had heard it all before but even so her heart hammered in her chest. It was for real now; there was no going back. Briefly she felt a stab of longing for her past life as Amelia, smart, successful and submissive. But life as ninety-seven in the de Groncourt stable was going to be nothing if not interesting. And the arenas were coming ever closer.

The doctor was speaking again.

"My lady does not brand. She feels that it might have a deleterious effect on your value if you ever do need to be sold. And besides," and here she smiled as she began to walk behind Amelia, "she feels that they are superficial compared to what she intends for you all."

Amelia was thunderstruck and as a consequence hardly felt the chip being implanted into the nape of her neck.

A brand being too superficial?

The guard had almost to support her to the tongue ringing, Amelia's knees would hardly take her weight. She was terrified of what was going to be done to her instead of branding.

As it turned out, she didn't find out that day or for the next few weeks and by the time she did, it was far too late.

Three male guards had set up a sort of assembly line for the ringing in a room just down the corridor. While the guard who had brought her twisted her arm up behind her back to hold her steady, the first man injected her with a local anaesthetic directly into her tongue, she was held for a few seconds, then moved along to where the second man reached for her mouth with forceps. And for all her determination that this was the life she wanted, Amelia broke and began to struggle. There was something terrifying about the forceps stretching out her tongue and she could see the thick punch ready to drive a hole through it. Much thicker than any she had seen before.

The guard was strong however and held her, forcing her head down onto the table, where the man held it. Then she reached under Amelia, grabbed a nipple and twisted it savagely. Amelia couldn't hold in the yell of pain and the forceps darted in, pinched her tongue and pulled. Amelia closed her eyes as the huge punch descended. There was a horrible impact – almost like a real punch, but almost no pain and then, as she opened her eyes again, she saw the third man reach in with the ring, insert it and screw on the catch ball. It was done.

Even by the next day the ache was fading and in any case their training got underway in earnest and they had no time to dwell on the peculiar feel of the rings. And by the end of the third week they no longer had to report to the doctor twice a day to have the ring rotated and checked for infection.

Their owner was as good as her word with regard to flogging. That very evening, and every evening, the whole squad had to line up after training was over and one by one, until it was dark and the wind was bitter, they were tied to the whipping posts and given thirty lashes each. There was no attention paid to however many a slave might have taken as part and parcel of training. During the third week of training, that meant that Diane and Amelia fared very ill indeed and were heavily marked for some time as a result. And the consequence of *that* was that they took even more punishment during their fourth week.

All the slaves trained for three weeks out of four and during the fourth week they paid for their keep by having what Angel called an 'on your back, week'. The slaves whose numbers were seventy-five up to a hundred went for their 'on their back, week' during their fourth week with the stable. It meant that they were shipped off to the capital city of the tiny, corrupt state in which the stable was located and put into a very select brothel. When the customers saw what marks Amelia and Diane carried, they correctly assumed that management would have no problem with them adding to them generously.

But the first week was dominated by the punishment of the unfortunate blonde American. During their early training when they were drilled in the basic moves involved in fighting with whips, pulling logs and wrestling, they were often marched past the grille in the ground that covered the pit the girl was in. They could look down into its depths – about eight feet, Amelia reckoned - and see the huddled figure on the four foot square floor. She was given enough food to sustain her but what shocked Amelia was the gleeful way in which the other slaves would add to her misery by urinating on her. But by the end of the week she began to understand. It was a way of indicating loyalty to Angel and their owner, reassuring them that they wouldn't behave badly and at the same time, they derived pleasure from having someone worse off than themselves, just as Angel had said.

When at last she was taken out, a bedraggled, shivering wreck, welted from neck to knees, she crawled in front of the whole squad to Angel's feet, kissed them and begged her to forgive her for having talked back to her and swore that she would behave from now on. Angel, who was standing beside Sadia with the squad forming a ring around them, did nothing for a second apart from continue her perennial habit of tapping her riding crop on the palm of one hand. Then, slowly and deliberately she lifted one foot and placed it on the back of the blonde's head, pushing it down to the ground. She maintained the pose for a few seconds and then let her up.

"Clean this wreck up and bring it to me at the house," she told the guards, then she and Sadia walked off arm in arm.

The other thing that occupied a lot of Amelia's time in the first week were the sleeping arrangements. They were far more random than she had imagined.

At the end of the day's training, the squad was simply divided into groups of twenty-five and the groups, no matter which slaves they contained were herded into the barrack houses. So for three nights in a row, Amelia found herself completely isolated from anyone in the batch she had arrived with. As a result she was in heavy demand as status was defined by who was first to have her and she was fought over continually and had to use her new ring on cunt after cunt. To make matters worse the days were becoming increasingly hot and dusty and the fatigue began to tell on her.

After three nights of nearly continual use, Amelia was dismayed when Angel had them out running in the endless scrub that surrounded the stockade and although she acquitted herself well, coming home in the top five along with Diane, when they had been rested, she had gratefully taken the water that had been passed around but had been unable to keep her eyes open and when the order to stand and be divided up for the barracks had been given to the squad, she and Diane had been found on the ground, fast asleep. Amelia only came round when two male guards grabbed her arms and dragged her away. Groggily she tried to work out where she was and what had happened, but it was too late for that. All she could focus on was Angel's voice.

"Both of them, three days' solitary!"

Amelia screamed when she heard the grate being lifted up and she was thrown into the pit, tumbling clumsily down, rebounding off the hard earth walls and landing in an undignified heap at the bottom. A few seconds later came the similar sounds of her fellow criminal being slung into another pit.

The only saving grace was that the weather was now no longer as chilly as it had been but that brought thirst to torment her where the only liquid available, between feeding times, was not what she cared to drink. It almost didn't come as too much of a surprise that the first of the slaves to pour a golden shower of their scorn over her was the American blonde. When the sun had been high on the first day of her punishment, she had squinted up at the bright squares of light where the sun struck through the grille and had seen the blonde grinning down at her and had known what was coming. The girl stuck out her tongue to show off her newly affixed ring and then slowly squatted down, allowing Amelia plenty of time to savour the sight of her shapely vulva with its wavy line of pearl pink inner lips between the plump cushions of her outer labia and the inviting globes of her backside, all things that were denied her in her solitude and which she now realised she missed at night. She longed for the feel of buttock flesh to squeeze, the outlines of welts to trace on soft breasts, and above all the rich taste of vaginas hungry for penetration. She lifted her face to the stream and accepted her stable's discipline.

As hers was a fairly short sentence, they didn't bother taking her out to hose her down and beat her as they had with the previous prisoner, she was just left to endure and her food and drinking water were lowered down to her. When she was lifted out finally, by means of a noose she fed round her torso while a guard hauled on the rope, she too had to abase herself at her trainer's feet and promise never to offend her again. As she did so and Diane cowered beside her, Amelia was quite well aware that it was inevitable she would offend again, simply because she would be told she had. She understood now that keeping the pits full was important to the psychological regime of the stable, and so it needed a constant supply of slaves kept in solitary, thus transgressions had to be found and the transgressors had to be seen to suffer.

As with the American, Angel told the guards to bring them to the house.

Still dripping from the hoses but deliciously clean at last, the two slaves were marched to the house as darkness fell. They were led by two of the male guards.

As yet none of the guards had used any of them; something which Amelia found odd, as her experience with other stables had been that constant access to the slaves was part of a guards' payment. But this time, as the rest of the squad were divided up into random groups for the barracks for the night, both men took their time about fixing leads to the rings in the cuffs that kept the girls' wrists together behind their backs and, as they fed the straps forwards between their legs, making them stand with their legs well apart, they took full advantage of the inviting cunt lips and the cunts themselves, feeling them with rough, thick fingers that made both girls wince as they clenched and twisted inside them. It seemed like a long time since Amelia had felt a man inside her, in any form. And she gathered by a fleeting glance from Diane that she felt the same. However, neither man said anything further or made any attempt to use them beyond the casual fingering and soon they straightened up and tugged on the leashes, taking the two girls towards the big stone house. Amelia shivered slightly as she felt the cool stone of the corridor under her bare feet as they passed the room where she had been chipped and then the tongue ringing room and finally came to a sort of office at the back of the ground floor.

Angel sat behind a huge, mahogany desk with Sadia perched beside her, one leg cocked up onto the desk, her skirt riding up farther than Amelia had ever seen before. The woman's legs were long and elegant and Amelia felt a twinge of longing for clean sheets, a comfortable bed and a long night alone with her. But the fact that her owner's arm was draped around Angel's shoulder, reminded her not to waste her time dreaming.

As she watched, Sadia's hand caressed Angel's cascade of blonde hair and then slid down the front of her shirt to gently run across the swell of her breast, making the trainer shiver with delight.

"I gather these two ran well today," she said to Angel as she withdrew her hand and stood up.

"Yes, I'll trial them in singles and in the chariots soon. With tits like hers, seventy-six might be a dressage candidate as well, if she can be disciplined enough in time."

Sadia came close to the two girls, who kept their eyes carefully lowered, and trailed the fingers of one hand across both their stomachs.

"Just keep whipping the sluts and they'll learn in time," she said, moving to stand behind them and trail her hand across their buttocks.

Angel stood up and came to stand in front of the two naked slaves. Amelia trembled in the close proximity of the two beings who had absolute power over her. And at the same time she felt herself moisten at the thought of the cruelties they were capable of. Her lowered eyes saw her trainer's hand reach out and one index finger begin to trace a circle round her left areola, causing the nipple to instantly harden and stand proud. Angel chuckled softly at the sight.

"Oh I will. I just hope they don't learn *too* quickly!"

Sadia laughed happily and summoned the two guards from the corners of the room, where they had stood since delivering Amelia and Diane.

"Enough business for one day," she said fondly to Angel. "I don't want you tiring yourself out worrying about these creatures." She turned to the men. "Take them to the rest room and prepare them."

The men bowed gravely and yanked on the leashes to turn the girls and took them to the foot of a flight of steps. As the men mounted ahead of them, so the leashes were dragged up into the crease of their vulvas and they struggled to keep up. Amelia's heart was pounding and she glanced across at Diane when they stood on the landing, wondering if she was as apprehensive as she ought to be. In Amelia's experience, something a dominant referred to as a rest room would probably be anything but. For a slave anyway.

But Diane was calmly looking about her and seemed unconcerned.

In the event it was just as bad as Amelia could have imagined.

They were led into a stone walled room with a plush, deep red carpet on the floor and electric candle lights in wrought iron sconces around the wall, to give the room a menacing, flickering light. Not that it needed to be any more menacing to the naked slaves being led into it.

At the nearest end stood two ornate chairs with intricately carved, bowed legs and backs, their cushions repeating the blood red colour of the carpet. The floor was scattered with chaises longues and ottomans with low tables between them while the walls were decorated with numerous chains and karabiners at raised-hand height and at ankle height. Ominously there were others slung from the ceiling beneath pulleys. And at the far end was a small, raised stage on which were two rectangular frames with chains at the corners and they were swaying gently at the ends of chains from two winches.

The guards pushed the girls towards the frames and one by one they were suspended inside them, arms and legs spread wide and tight to the corners, wrists and ankle cuffs linked to the chains. Amelia took a few seconds to come to terms with the stringent nature of her suspension before she looked up and saw that the winch from which the fame was suspended could run on rails out into the room.

The men left them and for a few moments the two hung in silence, the thick rings in their tongues preventing more than a comforting glance at one another.

Amelia reflected, with a mixture of bitterness and amusement, how much she had wanted to be taken to the dungeons of The Lodge – yet here she was filled with apprehension at the approach of the unknown in a dungeon that promised just as much deliciously erotic pain.

Before their limbs could ache too much, the door was flung open and Angel and Sadia entered.

They were dressed in long, scarlet gowns that opened at the front as they walked to reveal stocking clad legs and naked loins, the black and blonde pubes contrasting as the women kept close together. Above the waist the gowns flared open and just clothed the shoulders and arms, leaving the torsos caressed by tight black basques that pressed the breasts up until they were voluptuous mounds that threatened to overspill the cups. Their lips were heavily made up with scarlet lipstick t5hat made them look cruel and stern rather than glamorous. Behind them came the guards. The men were stripped to the waist and wearing black leggings and boots; the women stockings and basques like their mistresses. But what immediately caught Amelia's eye and made her heart skip a beat was that each man's cock swung free and naked as the leggings had cut out panels at the front.

When the procession had entered fully and the door was closed, owner and trainer, flung themselves down on the throne-like chairs, Angel immediately throwing one leg over an arm and reaching her hand down to start frigging herself. Some of the men carried bottles of wine and some of the women glasses, these they set down and when all the glasses had been filled they drank a toast to Sadie, who acknowledged it by draining her own glass and then standing up.

"My friends," she started, holding up her hand for silence. "I have great news and we have a cause to celebrate! The Owners' Council have just confirmed that the event at Bakhtar will definitely take place and the result will stand as a fully recognised one!"

Amelia knew the importance of this; it meant that win or lose, the black and yellow stable was a fully recognised stable now. Someone had been doing some serious negotiation, she guessed. But it also meant, she realised, that both stables would be going flat out to win. Sadie's to prove the Girl Squad's trainer, owner and methods were up to the mark and the Bakhtar stable would stop at nothing to avoid being beaten. She knew of the Prince of Bakhtar by repute – one of the cruellest and harshest Owners on the circuit – and she knew the stadium. It was where she had met Brian.

"Now I suggest we settle down to some well earned relaxation with these sluts!" Sadia was saying from the other end of the room.

"But will two of them be enough?" a male voice enquired.

Sadia shrugged and resumed her seat, caressing Angel's right breast. "If not, send down for more!"

CHAPTER 13

To begin with it was predictable. Two of the male guards stood behind the two slaves and performed a hard flogging for the amusement of the audience. Backs already sore from the constant beating in any case, the two recipients gasped and cried their way through it, hardly able to do more than make the slightest of twists in response to the heavy blows.

Amelia found the pain and the exposure a heady mix and even as her eyes closed in approaching ecstasy as the count mounted through the forties, she saw the couplings on the chaises longues and ottomans.

She climaxed just before the beating stopped and looked across at Diane who was just finishing twitching in the aftermath of her orgasm. The two flagellators stood back and were applauded.

Then two women hauled themselves up from where they had been sprawled under men who had fucked them in time to the beating and approached the stage.

Blearily Amelia watched them approach and saw the lengths of cord they were holding. Making an effort to revive herself a little, Amelia shook her hair out of her eyes and tried to take an interest in what was going to be done to her next. Swiftly the woman who had approached her made a loop with her cord, trapped Amelia's right breast within it and pulled the cord tight. It was a long time since she had been breast bound and she gasped at the strength of the erotic charge she got from the feeling of tightness and restraint, which only made her breast swell even more. She was admiring the way the right nipple was throbbing harder and harder into erection when the left breast was bound as well and Amelia cried out in pained delight. Vaguely she heard Diane react similarly beside her but then her attention returned to the guard whose basque had slipped while she was being fucked and now exposed two quivering mountains of white breastflesh crowned with hard pink nipples. Amelia longed to be allowed to get her mouth around them. But she turned and caught something one of the men threw to her and Amelia knew with one look that it was going to be a very long night.

It was a whip such as she had seen and frequently used at The Lodge, small but with stiff, square cut lashes. It was a devil when applied to breasts and cunts. The guard came forwards, making sure Amelia could see the whip and squeezed her tits.

"Let's give 'em a few more minutes to tighten up. Then you'll let everyone hear how you can howl, I think."

Amelia could feel the pressure growing in her breasts now as she contemplated the wicked looking whip. Next to her, Diane, her tits being bigger, had been put to breast whipping sooner and the room echoed to her cries as everyone, Amelia included, watched the trussed, darkening bundles of breastmeat bounce and quiver on her chest as the whip slashed down.

With no warning the guard in front of Amelia pulled her whip hand back and Amelia drew her breath in and screwed her eyes up. But then she opened them wide and expelled her breath in a shocked gasp, the whip had been delivered in an uppercut that had slammed into her between her legs. A bitter, burning sting invaded her instantly and as the second lash landed she made the frame shake with her efforts to twist and flinch. At the third lash she joined her voice to Diane's and didn't hear the cheering and applause that greeted their screams.

Diane's guard switched to her cunt at about the same time that Amelia's moved to her breasts. By that time

Amelia was vaguely aware that her head was lolling and her entire body was awash in pain to the extent that she couldn't tell if she had come or not. The thumping, stinging impacts to her breasts were no more than an increase in sensory overload in smaller packages and she was even able to watch her breasts mark and darken even further with a kind of detached interest that she hadn't felt since some of the more devilish dungeon sessions at The Lodge.

At last it seemed as though the woman was satisfied that Amelia's breasts were satisfactorily marked and she pressed herself forward. With Amelia being spreadeagled she was slightly lower than the woman and so she was able to present her lavish tits directly to her mouth.

Amelia sucked in the hard, rubbery nubs, gratefully and used her new tongue ring to its best effect to flick and tease them as they were presented. She was rewarded almost immediately by contented moans from above her. She longed to have her hands free to explore the cunt that would undoubtedly be flooding at the woman's crotch but that was not to be.

The breasts were taken from her and screaming with laughter the woman fell backwards off the stage, pulled down by a male guard who immediately dragged her to a sofa and climbed onto her. Diane however was getting a rogering from a male guard who was standing directly in front of the frame.

Suddenly someone pushed Amelia's frame and, running on the rails in the ceiling it swayed and jerked forwards and she was sent careering out into the room. She was rocking and spinning sickeningly until someone else grabbed her and used the control panel that hung beside the frame to lower it and Amelia felt the bottom hit the floor and the whole frame tilt forwards; then stop. She was held at about forty-five degrees to the horizontal. A man ducked into the frame to stand before her. He was naked and his cock, glistening with recent discharge, reared in front of her face. He guided it down and she greedily sucked in its girth and pungency, rolling her head to show how much she appreciated being allowed to pleasure it and again using her tongue ring. Behind her another man – or maybe it was a strap-on, she had no way of telling – slid into her stinging cunt with no difficulty at all. The man in her mouth grabbed her hair and rammed himself into her with all the careless dominance that Amelia so wanted and her cunt responded by lubricating to the point where she could barely feel the penetration. In her mouth the cock swelled and jumped madly and she was swallowing as fast as she could to keep up with the splashes of sperm. Behind her, the shaft pulled out and she found out that it was real as she heard a man's cry of release and hot dollops of spunk rained down on her back.

A woman took the man's place at her mouth and while Amelia craned her face up to try and tongue as best she could, she reached underneath and crushed her tormented tits. Amelia yelled in pain and this was what was required.

"Scream up my cunt you whore!" the woman growled and twisted the breasts harder. Amelia yelled again. Someone started fucking her again, her breasts were volcanoes of erotic pain, she couldn't tell what was going on any more. Above her the woman orgasmed and spurted a gush of rich juices onto Amelia's tongue, then she was gone and a man was laughing as he began to untie the loops around her breasts. She yelled again as blood flowed back into them and filled the welts and the crushed capillaries.

The winch buzzed again and she was pulled upright once more. In front of her tear-blurred gaze was her owner. Her lipstick was smudged and her face gleamed with discharge, but her eyes were alight with an unholy glee as she surveyed Amelia's spreadeagled body.

Slowly she leaned in and Amelia watched her tongue come out. She held her breath, this was an honour she had seen no other slave accorded. Her owner's face came closer still and the tongue licked slowly over her chin, where spunk still clung, then she licked down her throat to where the sweat was trickling between her breasts. Amelia looked down and watched her, aware that the whole room had gone silent. Then she stood up and addressed Amelia, eye to eye.

"I shall taste you when you are brought to me fresh from the arena. I shall lick the sweat from your battered and bruised body and it will be the taste of victory!"

"Victory!" The cry rang out and glasses were refilled.

Amelia's frame was lowered again, and this time it was lowered so that she was laid on her back on the floor and was used by what felt like every single person in the room. Women sat on her face or knelt over it so they could punish her tits some more, men fucked her or wanked over her, or were wanked by the women. Angel would occasionally prowl through the gathering, hair tousled and eyes heavy lidded, she would grab a female guard and make off with her back to the great chairs. Once or twice she saw Diane hoisted high in her frame, her body gleaming with sweat and spunk and her skin thickly welted with criss crossing, red lines. She grew disorientated through continual use and from being hoisted up and spun round, then laid down or tilted forwards or backwards. The lash stung her time after time and she could do no more than throw her head back to acknowledge it and eventually not even that. So they concentrated on flogging her between her widespread thighs to 'liven her up' as she heard Angel's voice say from somewhere above her.

The last thing she could remember of the night, when she woke the following morning was the trainer looming over her and then lifting her gown while she turned away so she could settle over Amelia's face. Summoning all her remaining energy, she resolved to give the best service she could and, rolling her tongue, began one last passionate exploration of a vagina that had played host to many cocks and she was rewarded once again by a copious outpouring of tasty juice as she made her trainer climax.

No allowance was made for the two exhausted slaves the following day. They slept in a cell in the main house but rejoined the others for full training. By the end of the day, Diane was practically holding Amelia up as they were paired in whip duelling practice. The whips they used were now real, if not as heavy as full arena ones.

The days ground past and Amelia began to feel that, the day after the party excepted, she was becoming harder and faster. It also seemed as though the guards and instructors were keeping a close eye on their various charges because changes began to be made.

Diane and Amelia plus two others were sometimes taken to a different part of the stable's grounds and put into harness for racing practice while the rest of the squad were tied to the great ropes and whipped through mass log pulling sessions. Sometimes Amelia found herself, usually with Diane, put into the pens that were simply giant cages of mesh about ten feet high, and given one to one teaching about wrestling holds with a scarred, older man who threw them mercilessly and beat them carelessly but slowly taught them how to stay on their feet and make sure an opponent didn't.

Also the sleeping arrangements began to change. They became less random and Diane and Amelia often found themselves quartered together. Furthermore, the girls were often chained two to a bed to stop the quarrelling and scrapping that had gone on previously. The chains were long enough to allow for plenty of nocturnal pleasure but not for bed hopping.

By the end of their third week, Amelia and Diane were put into a two pony trap. With a bar running across their fronts, so that their hands could grip that and keep their backs bared to the whip, they were taught to work in unison. To work in complete harmony. Every step, every movement of the head in response to the reins had to be perfectly synchronised.

Amelia knew they were being groomed for dressage and naturally 'learned' very fast, but made enough mistakes to earn the lash frequently enough to match Diane.

They also began to race seriously against one another and eventually against the cream of the stable - the solo fighters. Every stable had them. They were the best; they would have the entire arenas to themselves as they fought with studded whips, or competed in the pursuit running or fought in the cages. In the racing they were the seeded competitors in the singles, couples and in the dressage but Amelia knew they weren't usually used so much these days in the six-slave racing chariots, where injuries were most likely.

But just as Amelia began to look forward to every day, rejoicing in the hot pain of the constant lashing and the achievements she was being forced to; they were taken away to the state brothel.

Twenty-five slaves – the batch who bore the numbers seventy-five upwards were loaded back into the truck that Amelia remembered so well and chained in place once more.

By the evening of that day they arrived at a beautiful old house set back from a main road behind high hedges and at the end of a sweeping drive. Amelia noticed the unfamiliar, faint noise of traffic, drifting across from the huge, iron gates and also noticed that there were a lot more guards in evidence, they were all male and all had stun guns at their waists.

The herd of naked girls was shepherded into the cavernous marble-floored entrance hall and lined up before a well built woman with glossy black hair that hung in shimmering waves to her shoulders and who wore an exquisite evening gown of pale green, heavily embroidered satin that rustled seductively as she walked. She passed down the line, taking in each of them from head to toe.

"You'll do," she said at last and then stood in front of the line and addressed them all, just as a gaggle of girls descended the stairs behind her, their high-heeled shoes making no noise on the plush carpet but clacking on the marble of the hall floor. They wore tightly fitting basques and stockings and some even wore short dresses and skirts. They chattered as they came until the woman shushed them and sent them scuttling to the back of the house.

"This is the state brothel, in case you didn't know and you will be privileged to serve those in highest authority while you are here. As Sadia's stable is partly state sponsored, you will be paying your rent with your bodies. And as the state already partly owns you, you are worth only the pleasure you give. Expect nothing but extreme use here. The girls you just saw are the full time staff and will serve the more trivial requirements of our guests. You, however, are here to provide them with entertainment that will fulfil their wildest fantasies. In short; just because you are not at an arena doesn't mean you are not arena slaves. You are just serving in a different arena. Sadia and Angel will be informed if any of you fail to deliver everything a bought and paid for slut should."

She waved them away and the guards who had been standing at either end of the line, herded them towards a door that opened beneath the sweeping staircase.

"Not those two!" the woman called after them. "I want them in the stables!"

Amelia looked around to find that she and Diane were being pointed at, and with a rush of apprehension-charged excitement she realised that the two of them were being singled out for special treatment.

Diane stuck her tongue out obediently when the tall, dark haired guard gestured to her mouth while holding a leash with a small karabiner on its end. It was the first time since her ring had been fitted that someone had actually wanted to clip a leash to it. Over the past few weeks she had realised that the torrent of events and experiences had completely washed away all vestiges of who she might once have been. Now she took every day, minute by minute and didn't question anything or try to look beyond the next bout of punishment or pleasure.

And the constant presence of the whip was something that she found she needed now, so complete was its domination of her every waking moment. Sadia and Angel, after the party at the house, were goddesses and she would gladly prostrate herself before them or before whoever they wanted her to submit to. She belonged to them and had no desire to be anywhere else. But even in this happy miasma that only the daily beatings could break – and then only right at the end when the pain was at its peak – she couldn't help noticing that she was being kept with the pretty English girl with the bobbed hair and almost elfin face. The one who had introduced herself as Amelia and appeared to know that they had been sold to an arena. And what was more, Diane was noticing that as their training advanced, Amelia seemed to be almost one step ahead of their driver when they were run as a pair – almost as if she knew what was required without having to be told. It was subtle and probably not noticeable to the driver but as the right of Diane's bit was joined directly to the left clip of the other girl's bit, she could feel her turn or begin to stretch into a trot just a second before the whip landed or the rein tugged.

But she refused to let these thoughts bother her. Their Mistresses were pleased with them and that was all that mattered, now all she had to do was stick out her tongue and be led like the docile creature she was so rapidly becoming. She found that as she was tugged towards the stables she adopted an odd sort of neck forward stance as she followed the leash, her tongue helplessly pulled out from between her teeth, and as she stole a glance sideways she saw the other girl doing the same and with a surge of erotic excitement she realised that it was exactly the way real horses walked on the rein.

However, that first evening was the high point of the week and from then on it proved to be one of the most testing she could have imagined.

The next morning they were taken out early and scrubbed down by the guards with rough sponges that made their skins glow, then they were fed before being harnessed to a two seater trap like the one she had first learned her pony skills on. Her body could accept the harness with its straps and plugs now with no problem and she and Amelia stood with legs spread while the guards squatted in front of them and shoved the dildo and plug into each of them with only the most perfunctory of pauses while they screwed the plugs into the girls' anuses. Diane was thrilled with the actual harness as it was much more decorative than the workaday arena one. The strap that came across her stomach and to which the cupper was buckled at the back, bore a large silver oval that was engraved with some kind of crest – she supposed it was the crest of whatever country they were in. And by looking across at Amelia she could see that where her bridle divided into two straps at her forehead another engraved silver oval was fitted, and to finish off the ensemble, at the crown of their heads was a holder for plumes, and graceful feathers, dyed green, grey and black swayed above them, she could only assume that these were the colours of the country's flag. She felt her vagina heat and melt at the completeness of her owned status, she was not only owned by the stable but also by a country! And as the madam of the brothel had said, her only worth lay in the pleasure she could give to the people who owned her – who were *the* people! Or those who the government said could use her.

For the rest of that day and for the week they pulled guests around the park that surrounded the big house. The first day was typical of the rest. They were driven to stand beside the front doors of the house and were tethered by their tongue rings to a hitching rail. Eventually, when the boredom was finally becoming acute and her back almost aching with longing for the lash, several long, black limousines slid up to the front of the house and disgorged distinguished looking men in dark suits, accompanied by other men in sunglasses with suspicious bulges under their jacket shoulders. Even to Diane peering from between her blinkers, they screamed government, mobsters and minders. The women who accompanied them had the unmistakable look of secretaries and mistresses and some clearly fulfilled both roles.

Oddly enough it was the women who were most quickly drawn to the ponies and Diane found it deeply pleasurable to be admired and petted rather than beaten to work immediately, although she was never in any doubt that that would happen in due course.

The women spoke no English and she found it especially arousing that she couldn't understand a word that was being said about her, just as if she were truly an animal.

Small, delicate fingers, beringed and jewelled crawled over her skin, occasionally tickling her or scratching. Both she and Amelia stamped and fidgeted when that happened and gales of laughter erupted from the women, who then carried on just as if nothing had happened.

They pulled at the crupper strap and pulled her labia to one side, gasping at the size of the dildo she carried and giggling wildly at the discovery. One of them discovered Amelia's butt plug at the end of her tail and again the brightly dressed crowd stood closely observing one of their number who pried the object sideways so they could peer in and see how the plug was stuffed into the rectum.

Fingers were inserted between Diane's breasts and the straps that held the roots firm, she was scratched by rings several times and cavilled, tugging at her leash. One of the women smacked her bottom and said something that made the others laugh. Then inevitably the fingers began to trace the lines and bruises left by the whips and the way they led over the ponies' shoulders and down onto their breasts and the way they tracked across the buttocks and hips. Diane felt the fingers begin to become spiteful and clench in her buttock flesh. Again she stamped and fidgeted and was smacked, but at last a man called for them from the front door and they were left alone once more.

She had no way of knowing exactly what went on inside the house during the time they waited but eventually some of the party came back outside. The men's shirts were undone and their ties askew, the women's dresses were rumpled and their hair was tousled. But as one of the men came to the rail and unhitched them, from between her blinkers Diane could see an evil light in his eye and she could smell the alcohol on his breath. Behind her she felt someone take their place on the seat, then another jerk as the man sat down heavily.

One of the guards who had tacked them up earlier on came round from behind the house and after a brief conversation which obviously involved them the whip landed in earnest.

It came in heavy overhand throws, back and forth. It was the arena driving whip with a weighted tip – normally used to fetch the last drop of speed from a racing pair but never usually used to start them up – and it slapped hard across their backs. Diane found herself launching forwards, arching and twisting, colliding with Amelia and stumbling in her haste to escape the pain. But the pain simply followed. The girls could hear laughter and shouts of glee from behind them as the whip continued to fall.

What was worst of all was that the man was totally inaccurate and indiscriminate in his beating. Diane once felt the tail almost trip her up as it swirled across the fronts of her knees but fortunately the tip hit Amelia and failed to coil itself lethally around Diane's legs, trapping them and bringing her down.

Wide eyed and panicked, Diane galloped for her life as the hiss and smack of the lash filled her ears and the impacts almost dazzled her with bright bolts of pain. Time and again the unison and co-ordination that the pair had had beaten into them was undone by the sheer random sadism of the driver and the ponies' shoulders collided or their flying legs kicked each other as they sought to avoid the lash.

Only when saliva was flying over their shoulders and their mouths were gaping open so much that their bits were rattling their teeth, did the nightmare stop and the reins were savagely dragged back, making them rear so hard their feet nearly went from under them.

They were back outside the front door and a crowd was waiting for them. The couple behind them jumped down, flushed and excited by their ride, chattering loudly with their colleagues, and two more immediately jumped aboard.

Without a backward look the couple who had dismounted ran back into the house and Diane just had a fleeting pang of pity for her fellow slaves inside, there would be no let up for them until their users were exhausted.

Fortunately for her and Amelia, the tall guard from the stables was on hand and he seemed to have some authority. He checked them over, running hands over their quivering thighs and flanks, examining the state of their backs. He waved his hand and it was plain that he was putting them off limits for the moment.

But it was purely for the moment. As soon as he could feel their heart beats back to normal he let another pair drive them.

Both of them were cut in places by the time they were stabled that night. But simple plasters were applied the next day and they were put back to work, that being considered all a slave needed in the way of protection.

And so it went on till the end of the week. Each day brought a new load of people eager to sample the joys of driving the ponies part-owned by their state.

Diane considered that no person in the world could be as exhausted and desperate as she was by the time they were led out on tongue rings and taken to the blessed haven of the truck.

But then she saw the others being brought out of the house. They were all being carried and were simply slung down onto the straw-covered floor of the interior. There was no need for any chains.

Diane looked at the bodies before her as the truck pulled away and groggily the girls began to heave themselves up.

She gazed in awe-struck admiration at the tallies of welts she saw around her – and the traces of pin wheels and needles and clamps. Several eased themselves against the sides and sat wide legged, letting cool air circulate before they explored their own cunts; pulling their lips apart and craning their heads down to try and see if the marks – from where she sat, Diane could see the tell tale traces of needle play – were still there. Some stayed face down in the straw, their buttocks bruised dark blue and almost black by the canes. Next to her the Siberian girl, sporting spectacularly marked breasts, reached out and smiled as she traced some of the deeper welts from the lash across Diane's breasts and then the dent the weight had carved, making her suddenly proud of her mistreatment and her endurance. Soon the expressions of rueful sympathy for war wounds and admiration for each other's fortitude was in full spate by gesture and touch.

By the time they arrived back at the stable, there was a definite atmosphere of camaraderie; of affliction having been borne and conquered by stubborn endurance. For once arms were draped around shoulders without any thought of sex being entertained.

When the truck doors were flung open and Angel sprang up into the interior, holding her riding crop as usual, she stood for a few seconds looking down at the battered cargo. Then she grinned.

"Now you've got some idea of what you'll feel like after three days in an arena."

Strangely enough, Diane felt nothing but a calm acceptance of the challenge.

CHAPTER 14

There were four weeks left before the games in Bakhtar and Angel assured them there would be no brothel duty until after that. Amelia's attitude to her stable underwent a huge change in the following days. Prior to the brothel week, she had just been glad to belong to a stable, to be an arena slave and to be scheduled to perform before the crowds in Bakhtar. But now she was determined to do everything in her power to see that her stable would win.

She had felt the camaraderie on the way back from the brothel, she had also felt the growing bond between her and Diane as they ran between the shafts, the cruelty had never once made either of them falter or flinch from their duty.

To that was added her admiration for the psychology of the training regime. The whip and the pits had been used to subdue them, then the brothel's harshness had welded them together in their suffering and they were proud of how much they could take.

Now came the real business of honing skills.

The whips used in training more closely resembled full arena gear and the punishment lash was hardly used at all. For hours Angel had them facing each other in lines and practising holds and throws. From watching Carlo train the CSL slaves, Amelia had seen the crotch throw and had a head start at putting it into practice. She had an amusing couple of days effortlessly throwing her opponents until they learned it too and inevitably the day came when she found herself teetering on the hand of an opponent whose thumb was embedded in her vagina and whose finger was in her rectum, before being lifted clear off her feet and thrown heavily to the ground.

And here she found another source of excitement. Previously, she had only ever been an observer, but now she experienced the warmth and solidity of a female body struggling against hers. And now she really learned how to grip a breast and how a nipple could be such a deliciously weak spot on any girl, she learned how to lift a girl by her buttocks and let her fall, spread legged onto an outstretched knee, she found she adored the way the shock waves rippled through the female body as it hit the dirt. She loved the feeling of the softness of defeat in a body under her, panting in exhaustion, unable to rise or fight anymore, its tongue questing for her cunt to signal submission.

She loved tricking an opponent into lunging forward in a whip duel, only for her to skip backwards and strike hard down the back, dance away and then club the breasts backhanded with the lash as the victim arched in pain. She was quick to learn how to step in and trip an opponent, using the whip handle as a club to stun them or wind them first.

She watched in naked envy as those picked for boxing were strapped into the studded corsets and thongs – the studs facing inwards. The Siberian girl and the two Americans from her batch were all picked and when the rest of the squad were allowed to watch the practice bouts, Amelia joined her groans – part sympathy, part envy - to those of her colleagues when a solid punch was dug in to the body or crotch and the recipient would blink and shudder for a moment but then wade forwards again, desperately shrugging off the masochistic urge to invite more punishment so as to achieve orgasm.

Her own destiny however, seemed mainly to lie in racing and she and Diane spent more and more time in running single chariots, pairs and dressage – both singly and together.

Around her she could see that Angel and Sadia were encouraging closer and closer liaisons between the girls. Amelia and Diane almost always slept together and Amelia certainly had no quarrels with that arrangement, she adored Diane's breasts and for her part, Amelia thought smugly, Diane seemed to be very fond of the taste of Amelia's cunt. The two Americans who showed real boxing ability were often bedded down together, the Siberian and a Scandinavian girl who were both tough and big and who stood back to back and took on all comers with the whips, were an item. And so it went on.

Again Amelia approved. When it all came down to the final few points after three days of competing; having a lover to fight for could make all the difference.

Most frequently nowadays, the games would end in a mass melee, when the two entire stables were flung into battle against each other with some sort of objective or trophy for one team to try and take from the other. Once it had been judged which team had won, often the male guards were let loose on both teams in a final spectacle of debauchery that finally slaked the crowd's lust for sex, pain and conflict. And it was sometimes in that maelstrom of naked female combat that the outcome of an entire contest was decided – and there the ability to stand and fight for one another could be vital. Amelia watched the management of the squad with growing admiration and her determination to help the Girl Squad succeed hardened by the day

In the final few days, they practised with the six-slave chariot and in a high risk manoeuvre that Amelia knew would have provoked arguments long into the nights, the stable ran two chariots using the solo fighters. It was a measure of either Sadia's or Angel's will to hazard everything. It was unlikely the opposition would follow suit and so it might sew up the chariot races for the Girl Squad, but at what cost when it came to the single combats and racing if there were any injuries was the nature of the gamble.

And it was then, as they were being tacked up and Diane was clearly alarmed and unsettled as, for the very first time they were taken into their home arena, that Sadia whispered encouragement to them.

Angel was striding up and down the start line and addressing the drivers and whipmen. Both drivers were female – another first – but it made perfect sense to Amelia, they were light and strong after all, the whipmen were drawn from the more slightly built of the male guards.

"Just sprint them to the turns then rein them in! Understand? Don't! And I mean don't, try and race the corners yet! Just turn them gently and sprint them back up. Let me see how they go before we do any clever stuff."

A long wooden fence ran down the centre of the arena floor to make it serve as a racing track, most stables now had purpose built circuses but Amelia guessed Eric had balked at that extravagance for the moment.

The six-slave chariot was the fastest formation anyone had come up with to date. It consisted of a lightweight, aluminium body, big enough for driver and whipman, both standing, and a long shaft with two crosspieces. The first was quite short and took one slave on each side of the main shaft. At the front a wider crosspiece was affixed and here four slaves ran abreast. All four were connected by their reins, bit joined to bit, so that only the outside two had reins leading back to the driver. This made it simpler to steer the rig. The outside two slaves ran with steel gauntlets on their forearms and also wore light helmets to guard them from the lashes of the opposing driver, who would try to damage them as the rigs closed. The two outer ones were also only tethered to the crosspiece by one hand, their outboard one was free to hit the opposing team.

The other four slaves were the engine room. They just had to power the rig as hard as they could be driven to it. Amelia's and Diane's post at the first crosspiece meant that they were the responsibility of the driver to whip. The actual whipman had the highly skilled job of lashing the front team at full tilt, keeping them there and keeping them concentrating on the job in the crush and chaos of a real chariot race. He also was expected to try and trip or distract the opposition's front four.

What surprised Amelia was that she and Diane were rather more slightly built than was normal. But looking across to the second of the stable's chariots, Amelia could see that it appeared to be a deliberate tactic on Angel's part. She had two of her solo fighters on each team, manning the combat positions on the outside of the front crosspiece and the rest of the teams all seemed generally lighter than normal. She was going for speed and skill; gambling that they could run themselves away from the spectacular crashes and fights that the crowds loved to watch. While Amelia was taking all this in, a female guard had clipped her wrists to the shaft, checked her breast strapping was properly in place and that the narrow strapping at her groin afforded the minimum of protection allowed by the Owners' Council, from the enemy's whips and all of a sudden Sadia was there.

Amelia started when the woman stroked her hair and patted her flank and then reached over to do the same to Diane.

"You're my talismans, you two," she whispered. "My two last buys, you're going to bring me luck, I can feel it! Run like the wind my lovelies and bring me back the victory!" Then she was gone as suddenly as she had come.

"Alright! Let's get some order here!" Angel called as the guards pushed the front fours of the teams back to stand just behind the start line.

Satisfied, she stood back and fired her starting pistol which echoed thunderously in the empty stadium but even before the echoes had died, Amelia was furiously digging her feet into the packed earth of the ground, trying for every pound of thrust she could manage as the drivers yelled and the lashes thudded and smacked all around. She hardly noticed the ones that fell on her until she felt the front four ease back as their reins were pulled and the rig swung easily around to the right.

Then they were pounding down the back straight, all Amelia could see was the ground flashing past beneath her as the lash brought its familiar and welcome sting to her back. Then once more she felt the drive slacken as the front four were reined in and she and Diane exchanged fierce smiles as they swung round to stand at the starting line again. It had felt so good, they had gone fast enough to feel the wind in their hair and made the chariot leap and jerk behind them.

Angel was consulting a stopwatch with the drivers and whipmen who had leapt off as the rigs had skidded to a stop, while guards came forwards to hold the bridles of both front four teams.

Angel looked up suddenly and waved the drivers and whipmen back to their posts, Amelia felt the chariot shake behind her as they jumped on board.

"Okay! They've had a warm up lap, now work the bitches! Next lap we'll add the arsefire!"

Amelia smiled grimly behind her bit. She had often mixed up Carlo's special brew – as he called it – to rub into racing slaves' arses before they ran and she knew what went into it. Each stable had its own, jealously guarded secret recipe and by the sound of it, Angel's 'arsefire' was going to be worth a good few points.

The second lap was noticeably faster as the whippers' and drivers' arms had warmed up as well as the slaves. This time they cornered more quickly and Amelia felt the chariot drift out behind them as they swung hard round and started on the home straight at a slight angle which the driver corrected quickly.

Back at the starting line, Angel seemed relatively pleased and chatted easily with her staff as they set about bending the slaves over the crosspieces, unbuckling their cruppers and coating their butt plugs with a thick paste that reeked of ginger amongst other things. Amelia had frequently enjoyed screwing the butt plug back and buckling the crupper back firmly at CSL and had watched the ensuing prancing and fidgeting that followed a good application of Carlo's brew as evidence of a job well done. Now she gritted her teeth and waited for the effects of Angel's elixir to kick in. Beside her Diane suddenly let out a strange whinnying sound and began jumping, she glanced round and then gasped round her bit as a fire began to burn deep in her belly and most especially at her arse. Around her, heads tossed and feet stamped in both teams.

A guard brought out a plastic barrel of water with a pump operated nozzle attached and made sure the slaves all saw it.

"Two laps this time and if I don't see at least two seconds shaved off each lap time, we'll run 'em again!"

Amelia could hardly stand still by then. Her entire bottom was on fire and she couldn't wait to show Angel just how fast she could go! She would break the sound barrier if it meant pleasing her enough to allow the nozzle to sluice her rectum out and save them from having to run again with the arsefire still inside.

The pistol sounded again and if she had thought she had been trying before, Amelia realised she had been only trotting. The rigs were round the first turn almost before the lashes had bitten more than twice. She distinctly felt the inside wheel of the chariot lift as they cornered all four times. She ran with her eyes screwed tightly shut, just concentrating every ounce of effort into powering the chariot forwards and when she felt the crosspiece she was shackled to dig into her stomach as the front four were reined in, her legs almost went from under as reaction to the effort kicked in. And still her stomach and anus burned out of control.

"Okay, sluice them out and stand them down. Good run everybody! Nicely driven and excellent whipping. Of course on the day we'll increase the chilli powder so don't forget to hold on tight at the start!"

Amelia couldn't help a sob as she heard that, twisting, hopping and groaning at her station as she waited for her turn with the douche.

The sixty-nines that she and Diane indulged in that night – and the subsequent ones leading up to their departure for Bakhtar – were long and tender, with tongues lingering gently around the abused anal orifices before the vaginas were attended to and well-earned orgasms echoed softly around the rustling, moaning and mewing darkness of the barracks.

Then one morning they were woken by the shattering roar of a large plane flying very low overhead, shattering their sleep and startling them all into sitting bolt upright in bed as it came ear-splittingly low and then passed. Amelia looked around her naked and sleep-tousled barracks and realised that their transport had arrived. The girls all looked at one another, realising how desirable they all looked and at the same time realising that in a few days' time, they wouldn't look quite so fresh and bright-eyed.

The Girl Squad was about to go into battle for the first time.

CHAPTER 15

Diane looked down at her breasts. She was proud of them and knew they looked good both unmarked and, more importantly, with whip marks scoring them. Now however, they were squeezed between steel bars and passers by were idly pinching and twisting the nipples as they examined her. Some were feeling her shoulders and upper arms and thighs, and were discussing her likely stamina and pain thresholds before placing bets on the stable as a whole and on her in various events that apparently she was scheduled to take part in.

She tried to ignore the crowds and look around her at the Bakhtar arena. The banks of seats rose high and steep on every side and hanging from the roof that shaded some of the terraces were giant video screens that would relay the action from the arena floor in huge images that would satisfy the crowd's hunger for witnessing naked female combat.

She felt her pulse quicken at the thought of what would go on inside this stadium over the next few days. Even before her enslavement – her state of innocence as she now thought of it – she had heard rumours of what went on in these arenas in far flung corners of the world. And from what she had heard, the terraces were as much a sexual cauldron as the arena floors. But whereas before she would have been shocked and horrified at what was going on around her now, at present all she could feel was a sense of excited anticipation, mixed with anxiety that she might let Angel and Sadia down.

But beside her there was the calming presence of Amelia. Somehow nothing seemed to disturb her or upset her, it was almost as if she had been here before and knew all the ropes already. On the huge plane they had flown in on, chained in two long lines down either side of the fuselage, naked bottoms getting numb on the steel floor, Amelia had looked across at her and given her that fierce little smile they exchanged once they had been blinkered and were ready to race as a pair or as the first rank of one of the big chariots.

That had helped keep her calm during the long flight. Then they had been brought from an airfield over bumpy, potholed roads up into bare, rocky foothills and driven through a luxurious collection of hotels above a harbour and then deposited in barracks at the arena itself.

A whole day had dragged by with them chained in the harsh barracks, trying to sleep on stone-hard beds. And now, early in the morning on the following day, they were being assessed by excited crowds who were gathering for the games that would start the next day. The crowd swirled and swarmed before her, all around the long narrow cage in which they were held and Diane almost laughed as she felt yet another hand feel its way up into her cunt and recalled how prim and proper she had felt at the strip club the night her world and her life had changed.

Someone reached between the bars and opened her mouth to examine her ring and her tongue and she revelled in the admiring commentary she heard from a woman about the rigidity of her nipples. Her teeth having passed muster, Diane tried to turn her head to look at Amelia, it was virtually the only movement available to her. The yellow and black slaves stood in a long line abreast, kept upright and immobile by the bars of the doors that pressed at their backs and the closeness of the bars at the front that squeezed her breasts between them.

To her dismay, Amelia didn't look her usual relaxed and happy self. There was a tall man standing in front of her and Diane saw tears on Amelia's cheeks.

Somewhere deep inside her, Amelia had known that this would happen. But she had just had to hope that it wouldn't happen so soon. But it had, and there was a kind of poetic justice to it that caught at her throat and made some unwelcome and unusual tears come to her eyes.

Bakhtar had been the stadium where she had met Brian – having plucked up courage to buy a ticket with the aim of finding a male to take her under his wing inside the arena. And it had been here, at the pre-games inspection of the teams that she had met him. At the time he was hoping to meet Carlo Suarez and ask for the job of assistant trainer and the marks that he had laid across her bottom had helped persuade Carlo to take him on. And that had led to the visits to The Lodge and the work as groom to the CSL stable that was the only stable to keep small and hire out especially talented slaves to other teams.

And now Brian stood before her.

"Jesus! Amelia! How the....I mean where did you go!? We've been looking! Are you alright?"

She managed to nod and to stick out her tongue to show him her ring, which would explain more than words could in any case.

She saw him take in the sight and calm down a little.

"We got your letter of course, but no one could understand why you wanted to leave or where you would go. Look, just let me know you're okay and you're where you want to be and I'm okay with that."

Amelia nodded her head and Brian relaxed visibly.

"Good," he said.

"Brian!" It was a female voice and Amelia saw a blonde woman approach him; English to judge by her voice, immaculately dressed and it dawned on her that without her in tow, he had probably been snapped up by a scion of one of the wealthy families that inhabited The Lodge. She just hoped she was as submissive as he needed to make him happy.

"The yellow and blacks have got some damn good stock in the solo category! This could be a better match than we thought!"

She stopped when she saw him looking at her.

"Oh! That's that sub that disappeared isn't it? Was Carlo right and someone did snaffle it?"

Brian looked away, breaking the spell. "No, she's where she wants to be. And you know what Fi? I agree. I think this is going to be much closer than people think." He took her arm and they began to move away, but not before he glanced back and winked at her.

So people weren't giving them a chance. Right! Sadia's stable was going to show them! She turned her head to her right and saw Diane looking at her anxiously, having heard what had been said. She smiled encouragingly and Diane nodded, as if to say she had heard and understood.

In the cool of the evening the racing and dressage slaves were tacked up and paraded in their best harnesses and prizes were awarded for the best turned out.

Right from the start, honours were even.

Brian sat in the owner's box, just a few rows down from the Prince of Bakhtar himself and the Countess Sadia.

Down below – and up on the monitors in huge magnification – a whip melee was coming to its conclusion. Five of what everyone was now calling the Girl Squad had been pitched in against the same number of the prince's experienced squad. The result had been better than anyone had expected, the conflict had been long and hard and on the terraces there was a frantic orgy going on as the girls rolled in the dirt, clawing and raking at each other if their whips had gone. Punching and kicking, breast twisting and nipple tugging, the dust-covered furies provided superb entertainment, as welted flesh twisted and shone in amongst the clouds of dirt.

Gradually the action slowed as first one, then two, then more of the gladiatrices stood up to acknowledge the applause before sinking back down astride their defeated foes' faces. The cameras closed in on the foraging tongues licking up into the conquerors' cunts.

Anxiously he scanned the armbands of the victorious girls and saw that no fewer than three of them bore the yellow and black colours. Another girl went down under a ferocious volley of lashes, down onto hands and knees, her back shaking under the relentless barrage of lashes from above. She tried to rise but was beaten down again and ran out of strength, rolling over onto her back and flinging out her arms in defeat. Her victor held up her whip and then sank down over her face. That was four. All attention switched to the final duel where both girls had lost their whips and were wrestling. A hard upper cut that landed meatily between one girl's legs settled the issue. And it came from a yellow and black competitor. A draw. A good result.

Some of the downed girls were inert and guards ran on to pick them up and remove them before the next combat took place, which was scheduled to be a studded whip duel between two of the stables' solo fighters. Normally it was a spectacle he wouldn't miss but he had other business this time.

Beside him, Fi relaxed and took her hand away from where it had been rubbing at herself through the fabric of her light skirt.

"Wait here for me," he told her, knowing she needed no extra bidding. Studded whip fighting was always good entertainment value. She grinned up at him and lifted herself a little to hitch up her skirt. The hors d'oeuvres were over, now the real fun would begin.

Amelia champed her teeth on her bit as usual while her bridle was buckled at her neck and then settled herself into her wide legged stance to allow her groom to feed the crupper between her legs and feed the dildo and plug into her body. She had seen the dreaded arsefire spread on the plug and was praying the starting pistol wouldn't be delayed. She felt the usual stuffed sensation spread through her as the shafts nestled deep inside her and she waited anxiously for the fire to ignite. She was led quickly out into the dressage and single chariot race stadium and was shackled into her place while her driver climbed aboard and took his stance with the reins held tight against her neck straining forwards to balance himself. Her blinkers prevented her from seeing too much of the crowd apart from that bit of it sitting further down the straight. But right at the front a tall man forced his way through to stand right by the boarding beside the grass track. He smiled and gave her the thumbs up. She knew that the arena contests had got underway and assumed he was trying to give her good news.

In front of her the starter walked in front of all four chariots, Diane had been drawn in the outside lane, she in the inside, satisfied himself that all of them were behind the starting line and called to the drivers to set themselves and then the pistol sounded and she off. Her first proper event and she was determined to acquit herself well.

Her driver gave her only the usual amount of whip and she launched herself with her normal vigour into the race. But to her surprise her driver reined her in just a little halfway down the straight. She obeyed instantly of course but wondered how many laps the race would consist of.

Having been drawn on the inside, she rounded the first bend in the lead, running easily within herself and enjoying the colour and roar of the crowd. She listened hard to see if she could distinguish footsteps close to her but couldn't. She took the next bend equally easily, the whip just stinging her back enough to keep her concentrating and came back to the starting line. The whip was laid on a little harder and she accelerated down past the stand, the blinkers helping her ignore the distractions. Now she could hear the rumble of wheels on grass and made to accelerate again, but was reined in. She took the bottom bend and knew the other rigs would be closing on the inside lane as the stagger unwound and sure enough, she began to catch flickers of movement and hear ragged breathing from her left. For a whole lap nothing changed and she was still running easily but suddenly she got the 'hurry up' from her driver, he yelled and slammed the whip cord across her shoulders, hammering it down onto her breasts. She lunged forwards and charged at full tilt, having no way of knowing how far away the finish was. On her left there was definitely more noise now. Was Diane there? The whip came down across her back now. Keeping her at full tilt. She just had to hope. Round the bottom bend again and back onto the home straight but the finish line flashed past and she knew at least one more lap lay ahead. Saliva trailed from her chin and her breathing became heavier. The whip began to wrap her lower stomach and the top of her delta. She lifted her legs and maintained her sprint. Onto the straight once more and her driver began to shout more encouragement and the whip smacked her back, shoulders and stomach at random. Amelia knew it was the last lap and from somewhere pulled out more speed. And as she rounded the final bend, she found herself hoping Brian was still watching as she knew no one was in front of her.

Brian was impressed. He marked his card with the first and second place the Girl Squad had achieved in the first race as he made his way back to the arena.

Two pairs of solo fighters were slogging it out in the baking sun, even though it was early evening by then. Fi was on her knees to one of the prince's guards when he returned but that was not uncommon and he had no problem with it. She would be annoyed at missing the action below though and would be hurrying him to climax in her mouth.

Blood had been drawn and Fi had only just regained her seat, licking her lips and wiping her chin as daintily as she could, when the two Bakhtar girls went down. The cheering from the terraces was subdued by shock as the screens replayed the last few moves; the Countess's girls using their shields to knock their opponents' whips away and then flicking their own at the tops of their enemies' thighs, even through the leather cache sexes, the thumping impact was too much after the punishment they had already taken.

He and Fi walked down to watch the dressage in the evening as the arena emptied at the end of the first day.

Amelia and her companion performed a faultless routine, turning their rig on a sixpence, reversing and high stepping in total unison. Coming to one knee and bowing their plumed heads to the judges at the end of their routine, the crowd actually gave them a standing ovation. The Countess acknowledged the praise graciously and Brian gazed thoughtfully at the spectacular blonde sitting beside her. There had been rumours circulating about her. Angel, they called her. She would repay careful attention, he thought and dialled Carlo's number on his mobile.

He could have returned to the arena to watch the punishments being dished out to the losers, later in the evening. That was where the audience could play a part by giving the thumbs down until the punishment met their approval. The better show a girl had put on could lessen her tally, but on the whole the crowd just liked to settle down and watch prolonged flagellations.

The second day was divided between log pulling events in the arena and individual contests in the pens.

Again Brian was impressed by the way the Girl Squad pulled their huge log across the sand in such a steady, disciplined fashion. Log pulling was brutally simple. In the mass event almost the whole squad lined up ahead of a telegraph pole sized log with a coarse rope over their shoulders. They simply had to get it twice the length of the arena floor ahead of the opposition. The lines started by swaying from foot to foot, to get the weight moving and then they had to just lean and sweat under the lash until the job was done. The close ups of the sweat-gleaming thighs and backs being lashed almost without let up was the main attraction.

The Girl Squad won by inches and the prince stormed out of the owner's box. The lead was beginning to look ominous.

The Bakhtar stable managed a comeback by taking the paired log pulls, in which two slaves pulled one log for a length of the arena, then came back with two and finally toiled another length with three.

Meanwhile, at the racing track, Fi texted him to say that 'his' slave had won another single race and the Girl Squad as a whole had taken the event comfortably.

The paired racing was won by the Bakhtar stable however.

After the worst of the mid day heat had passed, Brian went to inspect the cages where the slaves due to fight in the pens were kept. Damp tarpaulins had been spread over them to keep them cool and Brian found Amelia, lying, relaxed and cool in the third one he tried. He managed to whisper the score to her before a guard moved him on and it obviously affected her as in her first wrestling bout she took out a heavily built black girl with a throw that flattened her against the bars of the pen. As the girl came back, snarling defiance, Amelia had ducked under a swinging fist, tripped her and then followed her down, lying on her back with one arm round her throat and the other hand squeezing the life out of a big mound of soft breast. The girl's buttocks had humped her deliciously but she had held on, rolled over, got her into a leg scissor hold and squeezed as hard as she could until she felt the girl weakening and then she had released her, pulled her to her feet and slammed her face first into the bars and pinned her down a she crashed backwards.

She looked up just as Diane landed a flying kick on her opponent and knocked her clean out.

She fought six bouts in quick succession and lost the last two. That meant some punishment in the evening session but being put to a whipping post held no terrors for her. The roars of approval as the beatings were carried out, at least ten separate punishments being carried out at any one time under the flood lights, were a real turn on and she watched herself up on the big screens, hardly able to believe how exciting it was to watch her own back suffer for the pleasure of the orgiastic crowd.

But best of all, when they were being led back to their barracks, Sadia had appeared and whispered to both her and Diane how pleased she was with her talismans.

The final day was given over to the six-slave chariot racing, the final solo contests in the arena and then the mass finale in the late afternoon.

Amelia's heart was thundering as she was shackled to her spar and her tack was checked by the opposition's drivers. She could see Diane was tense as well. But who wouldn't be? All round them the crowd yelled and cheered, a lot of yellow and black seemed to be in evidence and Angel was repeating to their whipman that the scores were close. They had the advantage but still needed to win the racing to be able to relax.

The first race was so fast that Amelia hardly noticed it. She didn't know if Angel had really meant it when she had threatened to add more chilli to the 'arsefire' but it certainly felt like it. The Girl Squad raced for the sanctuary of the buckets of water as if all the fiends of hell were at their heels. They came in third, but that was enough as the other chariot had won and first and third scored more highly than second and fourth. Their cruppers were unbuckled and the plugs slid out, cameras greedily following every scene and being cheered to the rafters by the crowd as giant images of shapely, whipped buttocks releasing their grips on greased plugs were flashed up.

But for the slaves the relief was short. They were sluiced out, given water to drink and rested for a few minutes and then re-harnessed for the second race. It was a longer one this time so thankfully there was no coating of the butt plugs. It would be sheer endurance.

As with her first single race, the driver kept their speed under control for the first two laps, letting the other rigs pull ahead. But on the third she made her move, yelling and wielding the whips in overhead throws, she and her whipman, lashed the team mercilessly, and the acceleration took the opposition by surprise. In the space of one length they had made up ground and as they rounded the corner at the end, their own whipman was able to distract the oppositions two fighters and trip one of the first row, nearly bringing the rig down and enabling them to slip past into third place. Now they could go hunting for the remaining Bakhtar rig and on the fourth lap the two Girl Squad chariots were able to squeeze it and the whips took the legs from under two of the front four. The crash was spectacular. The crosspiece at the front dug into the sand, making the entire rig somersault and throwing the driver and whipman clear. The driver landed almost under Amelia's feet and she stumbled and very nearly went down herself. Then they were past the wreck and both teams could canter safely for the line. Sadia's and Angel's gamble had worked, the extra speed and toughness of a light team coupled with solo fighters had taken the opposition by surprise and resulted in vital points at just the vital time.

As she sweated and shook in her harness while the guards came round with carefully rationed water, she was able to watch the crash in slow motion on the monitors. She had always enjoyed the chariot racing but to have actually been there and seen the dust clouds fly up as the girls slid off their feet, legs tangling with their team mates and the rig had tumbled majestically through the air with shrieking slaves still attached had been a high the like of which she had never experienced.

She watched as the bodies thumped down in slow motion and the breasts and buttocks rippled at the impact. Glancing back down to the track, she could hardly believe that Bakhtar could field two rigs for the final sprint. The slaves limped home and were immediately worked on with liniment and salve.

Angel was closeted close by with her drivers and whipmen.

"They'll go for a crash on the first lap. Steer clear at all costs!"

Then the guards came around with the wretched paste again and all Amelia could focus on was getting back as fast as possible.

The damaged rig targeted Amelia's and Diane's rig exactly as Angel had foreseen. Barely half way down the first lap, Amelia suddenly felt a heavier than normal lash blaze across her back and wrap her hip. Instinctively she twisted and broke her rhythm, slowing her side enough to make Diane rear her head as the rig dragged just a little. Diane's driver yelled something incomprehensible and suddenly Amelia was under a hail of lashes from two whips but the front four accelerated under the lash form their own driver and the rig drew ahead, but the corner approached and if they slowed down, the punishment would resume and sooner or later, someone would be tripped.

Their driver took the corner at full speed, risking all by letting the chariot go up onto one wheel but by dint of both occupants leaning well out to counter balance, they came round well ahead and the damaged team had no chance of catching up.

In the team changing rooms the mood was one of unrestrained joy. The guards unharnessed all the slaves as the cameras kept their lascivious watch and made no secret of their pleasure, fucking some of them, allowing others a mouthful of sperm. Even Angel fondled some of them, smiling more broadly than Amelia had ever seen her. She found herself and Diane ignored against one wall and she buried her face in Diane's breasts, making her lover moan and cry in abandoned pleasure. But then Sadia swept in, magnificent in a scarlet shift dress, exquisitely tailored to her lithe form. She shooed out the cameras and the disappointed boos from the crowd made everyone laugh out loud.

Their owner addressed the guards of course, but it was plain that she didn't mind the slaves hearing either.

"We've not only won, we've massacred them! The finale is now officially just for fun!"

There was a cheer from the guards but Sadia held her hand up.

"That does not mean however that we're going to take it easy! The Girl Squad is here to stay and I mean to make sure everyone knows it. We're going to beat them to a pulp.......and then you can have fun! Guys, fuck yourselves blind if you like! Girls, there's going to be a lot of cock out there, so make sure you all get your share! There's a wall been built across the centre of the arena. Both teams will race for it and the ones who get there first will hold it against the others, obviously with an advantage. We will win!"

Wrists were unclipped from behind backs and floggers with rounded metal studs set in the tails were handed out and Amelia just couldn't stop grinning as she jogged with her companions out through the tunnel and into the blinding light of the arena. She knew how this would go. They would race the Bakhtar team for the wall of earth that had been thrown up across the arena and if they won, they would defend it until the owners judged that the crowd had seen enough whip action and then they would allow the male guards on to flog and fuck the slaves of both stables into submission.

But the female guards attached to Sadia's stable were not going to miss out and Amelia found herself standing next to the woman who had driven her in the chariot races. She was trim and sinewy and grinned at the slaves around her.

"Let's make the boys work for it, girls!" she said.

"We're worth it!" came another female voice, and to Amelia's amazement, Angel, tall and blonde and heart-stoppingly sexy in her nudity was prowling behind the line of her stable slaves.

"Finish the sluts off quick and then let's have the guys brought on!"

From the tunnel behind them the naked male guards of both stables came out, whips held at their thighs, cocks waving slowly as they walked. Amelia couldn't wait to fight and lose to them, the opposition's girls would be a welcome warm up.

From up on the wall, a starting pistol fired and from both sides of the wall the two sets of slaves rushed forwards.

Amelia felt the sand beneath her feet and the warm wind in her streaming hair as she raced towards the climactic struggle; a struggle that would only end when every girl was down.

She was home at last!

Waving her whip over her head and shouting a wordless challenge to the world while the crowd shouted her on, Amelia went joyfully to work.

Membership of the Silver Moon readers' club is absolutely free!

You can order copies of Silver Moon, Silver Mink and Silver Mistress books from the privacy of your own home. And you can also pre-order new publications and receive a substantial discount!

There are always offers for members and you can receive books that aren't on offer in any bookshops like some of our illustrated books.

Just cut out this page and send it to;
Silver Moon Reader Services,
Suite 7, Mayden House,
Long Bennington Business Park,
Newark NG23 5DJ

Don't forget to include your own name and address and you'll receive our latest brochure and an order form, plus you'll get £3.00 off your first order!

Over the coming months you'll get reviews of books from other readers, be able to exchange letters with the editor, read interviews with your favourite authors and lots more!

Membership is free and your privacy is assured.